ADA VANE

LEAPS & LIES

Cover by Danielle Greaves

Editing by Maddi Leatherman of EJL Editing

Proofreading by Zee of the blue couch edits

First edition 2024

Contents

Author's Note

While *Leaps & Lies* is a *not* a dark romance, it does contain content that may be troubling for some readers, including: body shaming, disordered eating (not main character), explicit sexual content, physical injury (joint dislocation), and under-negotiated kink. If you have questions regarding this content, please contact the author.

Knowledge of ballet is not necessary to understand or enjoy *Leaps & Lies*. For readers interested in delving deeper into the world of ballet, the end of the book includes a glossary containing relevant ballet terms and conventions.

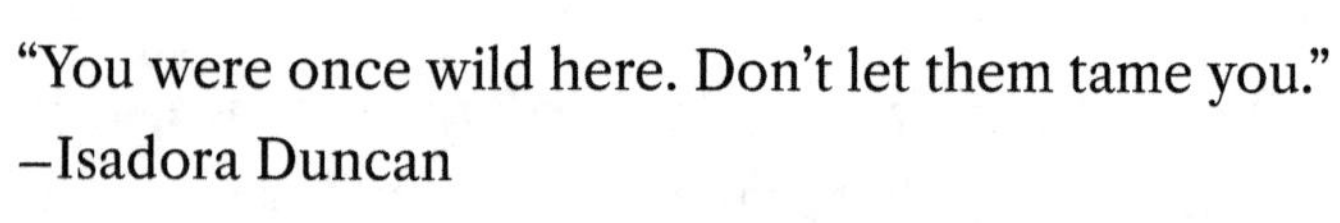

"You were once wild here. Don't let them tame you."
—Isadora Duncan

Part One

The Entrée

Chapter One

Vivian Ladoe didn't set out to be a liar. She simply never imagined that she'd make it through Ellapond Ballet Company's open audition. Despite being smaller and newer than some of the city's dance companies, Ellapond has quickly earned a reputation synonymous with excellence.

Sure, she moved to Bristol from Brighton Harbor with the singular goal of pursuing her ballet career. And yes, breaking into a newer company is easier than being cast by one of the city's ballet pillars, Mouveaux Dance, for example.

But still. The odds of being invited for a private audition were so slim during her open audition that Vivian never considered what to do if she saw **Ladoe, Vivian** on the callback section of EBC's website. She barely let herself imagine the possibility.

As she sits on her lumpy green couch in her shoebox studio apartment, Vivian stares at the email from Maureen in administration at Ellapond.

> *Thank you for your interest in joining the team at Ellapond Ballet Company. On behalf of our casting director, we invite you to join us for a company class. Please indicate which of the company classes you are available to attend.*

Vivian prefers not to call herself a liar, but as she stares at Maureen's email, a brick of anxiety settles in her stomach. It's a poorly kept secret that youth is a prized characteristic among dancers. Bright eyes, nimble limbs, and naive malleability make for beautiful ballerinas. Particularly from the perspective of choreographers and directors aiming to avoid the physical limitations and hefty price tags of seasoned professionals.

Ballet has always been Vivian's dream. The language of her soul. After twenty-four years of just scraping by, dance is *hers*. The thing that draws the line between surviving and living.

But auditioning in her age group is practically a death sentence. If she's lucky, Vivian *might* get a chance to be selected for the corps de ballet, but she'll have absolutely no shot at a more prestigious role. Even the newest dance company isn't going to risk casting her with no resume or portfolio as a soloist. As a no-name ballet dancer auditioning for the first time at twenty-four, she'll be lucky if they don't laugh her out of the company class.

By twenty-four, she should be on her way to the height of her career, not stepping onstage for the first time. Older dancers come with higher salary requirements, higher injury risks, and sometimes higher rates of drama. She understands why Ellapond would write her off. But she's never going to get onstage if she doesn't get in the door—any door.

With the weight of guilt pressing down on her shoulders and forming a pit in her stomach, Vivian emails Maureen to schedule her private audition during the YA (15–20) Company Class on Tuesday afternoon. *Here's hoping no one asks for her ID.*

Chapter Two

Vivian was on track to arrive early. She painstakingly chose an outfit. One that hopefully conveys hard work and elegance with a low maintenance attitude. An outfit that says, *Cast me as a soloist even though I'm a nobody in this city. Also, don't ask how old I am.* That's not too much to ask of an outfit solely consisting of tights, a leotard, and tulle masquerading as a skirt, is it?

She was on track to arrive early and ready. Ready being as warmed up as she could manage by doing jumps and stretches in the three square feet of empty floor space in her studio apartment.

Vivian was supposed to be early—until the driver's door of her geriatric, rusty silver Honda doesn't open.

She jams the key fob with her thumb again and listens as her car chirps back at her. The crackled silver paint of the door sizzles against her fingers after hours of sitting in the late August sun. The burning sensation is sharp, and Vivian flinches away. Sweat drips down her neck and loose pieces from her blonde ponytail are sticking to her shoulders unpleasantly. The car door still won't open.

Vivian checks the time. She's not late yet, but her margin for being early is dwindling fast.

Dropping her bag on the concrete, Vivian grabs the door with both hands and gives it one final, firm tug. The handle snaps clean off the door.

Fuck.

She's not going to cry. If she cries, she'll have to fix her makeup, and she *definitely* does not have time for that. Ellapond won't cast her if she's late because she cried her eyeliner off over a broken car door handle. What a stupid excuse.

Vivian needs this audition. She *needs* this audition. And she needs to get in her car if she has any hope of getting anywhere in this stupid city where she knows no one and no one knows her.

With a shaky sniffle, she tosses her handle into her bag and tries the one of the back door.

It opens on the first try. Of course, it does. Vivian stares at the driver's door longingly for a beat before she dumps her bag onto the back seat. Sighing, she scrambles, climbs, and wiggles her way inside the car, over the center console, and into the driver's seat. She checks the time again and starts the car. At least the casting director will have already arrived and won't see her climbing around inside her car akin to an unsupervised child in a supermarket parking lot.

Fuck.

Vivian pulls into Ellapond's parking lot late.

She's technically on time for the company class, but if there's one thing that dancers are neurotically specific about, it's schedules. Early is on time, on time is late, and if you're truly late—don't even bother. Timing is everything.

There's a flashy-looking black sports car idling in the spot next to her and it gives Vivian hope that maybe she isn't the only one running *late*. If it's the instructor or casting director, maybe she can sneak into the building before they notice that she hasn't arrived yet.

Shutting off her car, Vivian clambers over the center console and tumbles into her backseat. She rights herself, grabs her bag, and climbs out of the backseat with as much grace as she can manage. It's not much given that her sandal manages to get hooked on something and she practically face-plants onto the pavement.

"The women's shelter is over on 5th and West. Right next to the library."

The words sway into each other, a wave washing ashore, and it takes Vivian a beat to realize they're aimed at her.

"Sorry, do you need directions?" she asks on instinct.

When she's unstuck her sandal from the car, gathered her bag, and found the source of the voice, she immediately wishes she hadn't.

The car that was idling next to hers is now vacant, and there's a man staring down at her. As she glances at him, strands of hair cling to the back of her neck, and a bead of sweat trickles down her back beneath her leotard. It's way too warm for the layers she's wearing.

The shadow cast by the man's hat obstructs his face but if it's anything close to the rest of him, Vivian already knows it will be obnoxiously attractive. He's dressed casually in clothes that must have been perfectly tailored to his body. With arms that should be illegal and jeans that Vivian wants to peel off with her teeth, there's absolutely no reason for him to be glaring down at her in Ellapond's parking lot. Much less asking for directions to a women's shelter.

Are men even allowed to go to women's shelters?

"Do you need directions?" Vivian repeats, because what else is she supposed to say?

The man scoffs. "This is a private lot. You can't park here."

Okay, so much for hoping he might be attractive and kind. It's nice to have dreams.

Vivian peers down at her street clothes. With an oversized tee shirt that she's cut the neck out of and loose sweatpants that are ballooning over her sandals, chipped pink toenails barely peeking out beneath them, she doesn't look her best. Sure, she picked out her nicest leotard and a brand-new pair of tights for class. Her bag holds her favorite rehearsal skirt too, but all that glamour is hidden under loose clothes and a frizzy, unraveling ponytail that *apparently* make her look homeless. Appearance aside, this man, with his hat and his stupidly hot arms, still doesn't have to be rude . . .

"I know it's a private lot. I'm going inside." Vivian gestures to the building behind her before promptly turning and hustling toward it. She's not *technically* fleeing the scene, since climbing out of the back seat of your own car isn't a crime, but her cheeks heat all the same.

But she's going to be late-*late* if she stays to argue with Hat Guy.

Chapter Three

In the time it took Vivian to locate Maureen from administration, introduce herself, change out of her street clothes, twist her frizzy ponytail into an almost neat bun, and be ushered into Studio B for the YA (15–20) Company Class, Hat Guy had arrived. He stands at the front of the room talking to an intimidatingly beautiful blonde woman. They're speaking quietly enough that Vivian can't catch a single word from across the room, but her heart sinks into her stomach anyway.

The woman is wearing a long wrap skirt that could belong in a boardroom or next to a barre. Her white-blonde hair is smooth, and her posture is excellent. Despite the contrast of the woman's elegance with Hat Guy's casual attire, the blonde appears closer in age to Hat Guy than to Vivian. She's radiating a commanding and addictive energy. This woman could order Vivian to practice beats until her feet go numb and Vivian would thank her for the honor. In contrast, Hat Guy looms like a specter coming to haunt Vivian for her lies. With the brilliance of the August sun no longer blinding her, Vivian does her best to covertly study Hat Guy from across the room. With curly brown hair that's escaping from underneath his ball cap, a tall and lean frame, and thighs that fill out his jeans far too well, he's even more handsome than Vivian's initial assessment. It's devastating.

Together, Hat Guy and Blonde Lady make a beautifully impressive pair, statuesque at the front of the room.

"Today's class is being run by Ms. Renee. She also handles casting and choreography," Maureen gushes as she leads Vivian toward the pair. "Since we're a newer company, we wear several hats."

Maureen fiddles with her necklaces, and Vivian nods absently in response. If Ms. Renee is willing to believe that Vivian is nineteen, she doesn't care how many hats the other woman wears.

Studio B is littered with dancers along the perimeter in various states of stretching and dressing. Aside from the unfamiliar faces, it looks remarkably similar to every studio Vivian has seen on TV or online. Polished wood floor and sturdy barres lining two walls. The wall opposite the door is covered in floor-to-ceiling mirrors, and a folded, thick mat lies next to a built-in audio/stereo system.

It's far nicer than Brighton Harbor Dance back home, but it's built with the same bones. Familiar, but nicer in all the best ways. The square windows along the top of one wall allow the natural afternoon sun to shine in. Sunlight bounces off the white walls, basking the studio in an ethereal glow. Despite the August heat, the studio has a comfortable temperature that hints at the presence of air conditioning. It's a far cry from the tiny, humid basement ballet studio Vivian grew up in.

Vivian catches a few dancers throwing glances her way, but she doesn't react as Maureen continues to drag her across the room to Blonde Lady—Ms. Renee—and Hat Guy.

How does he know Ms. Renee? Does he work here? Are they together?

Maureen stops them in front of the pair with a warm hand on Vivian's shoulder.

"Renee, this is Vivian Ladoe. She's here for your 2:30 class."

Ms. Renee reaches a manicured hand out to Vivian and flashes a dazzling smile.

"Nice to meet you, Vivian. I watched your open audition, and I'm interested to see how you fare today."

Despite the polite handshake and smile, the words land as a challenge.

It doesn't matter. Vivian's here for a soloist role and Ms. Renee's dazzling, shark-like smile isn't going to stop that. Vivian knows in her bones that she can handle anything this woman throws her way.

"I appreciate the opportunity, Ms. Renee. I'm confident that you'll be happy with my performance."

It doesn't go unnoticed that neither Ms. Renee nor Maureen elects to introduce Hat Guy. In the bright fluorescents of Studio B, Vivian can finally inspect his face. It's indeed just as attractive as the rest of him. A strong bone structure frames a pair of green eyes, brown hair curls out from beneath his hat, and he boasts a jawline sharp enough that Vivian could use it to shave. On second thought, the idea of his jaw anywhere near her legs sounds fatal. She couldn't survive this man's face so close to her skin.

With one last cursory glance at Hat Guy's jawline, Vivian turns to Maureen.

"Thank you, Maureen. Is there any other information or paperwork you need from me?"

Vivian hates to ask. She's holding her beating heart in her bare hands and praying Maureen won't spear it by asking for her ID, but she *needs* to know. If everything is going to fall apart, let it happen now while she can still pretend this was all a comical accident.

Maureen smiles and her layered gold necklaces *clink* together. "Not right now. When Ms. Renee is done with you, we'll see if there's anything else I need."

It's clear that someone has carefully trained Maureen not to give anything away because she's deliberate with her words.

We'll see if there's anything else I need. We'll see if they cast you.

Maureen's doubt only solidifies the confidence in Vivian's gut.

"We're starting in five so please warm yourselves up enough to begin at the barre!" Ms. Renee calls to the room before turning to Vivian. "Do you need a warm-up or can you get ready for barre?"

Vivian doesn't bristle, but it's a near miss. "I'm fine, thank you."

"You can use any of the cubbies at the back of the room for your belongings. Pick one that isn't labeled."

Vivian nods at Ms. Renee and crosses the room to the tall shelves set against the wall next to the door. The room has emptied out some, the dancers from the earlier class gone and only about fifteen dancers remain. They're in various states of stretching and putting on shoes, leaning on the barres and quietly chatting.

She's hunting for an empty and unlabeled cubby when a bright voice chimes from her left. "There's one left next to mine if you want it."

A girl with shiny, dark chocolate-colored hair wrapped into a braided crown uses a water bottle to gesture at an empty cubby. "Some of the dancers get a little . . . possessive of their cubbies. Even when they aren't here to use them." The girl rolls her eyes, and Vivian immediately understands. There's a reason for the stereotype about dancers and divas.

"I'm Scarlett. It's been a while since we've had any newbies."

"Vivian. Thanks for the cubby tip, but I'm not new."

Scarlett raises a sculpted eyebrow, and Vivian immediately envies her flawless pale skin. She's beautiful in that tall, willowy way every dancer dreams of being. Scarlett appears younger than Vivian, but she's probably right around Vivian's fake age of nineteen.

"I'm new to the city and Ellapond but not *this*," Vivian says, gesturing to the studio with a pointe shoe in hand.

"Well, good luck either way. Ms. Renee is no joke," Scarlett answers.

Right on cue, Ms. Renee claps her hands and walks to the middle of the room.

"Just a quick announcement and then we'll begin at the barre."

When Vivian glances around the room, every dancer is gazing at Ms. Renee with rapt attention, devotees waiting for their gospel.

Vivian's going to dazzle this woman who has every dancer in the room hypnotized. She's going to dazzle Ms. Renee, and she's not going to pay any attention to Hat Guy, who is inexplicably *still* loitering in the corner.

"As you are aware, we are casting for our winter performance. By the end of the week, we expect to have all principal and soloist roles filled."

Out of the corner of her eye, Vivian can see Scarlett nodding. This must not be news to her.

"I am pleased to announce that Mr. Julian will be assisting with the production. Though he has been with us for only a few weeks as an artist-in-residence, he's performed countless pas de deux. His experience with partnering will be invaluable to this production."

When Ms. Renee gestures to Hat Guy—no, *Mr. Julian*—Vivian's heart sinks. If he's involved in casting, she has no hope of even making it into the corps de ballet.

"Please give him a warm welcome."

The room fills with polite applause.

Vivian's cheeks burn, and Mr. Julian nods.

Chapter Four

The company class flies by.

By the time it ends, Vivian is red-faced, breathless, and in need of new shoes. She thought she'd be able to get more time out of this pair, but the sharp stabs jittering up her toes say otherwise.

Since moving to the city, she's tried to practice as much as she can, but without a studio, it hasn't been easy. It's standard practice for companies to provide their dancers with shoes. But no studio and no company mean no new shoes. Instead, it means Vivian has tried every glue, tape, and sewing trick she knows to extend their life. Most professional dancers only get between ten and twenty hours out of their pointe shoes and Vivian tries not to think about the mileage on her current pair.

"Ms. Ladoe, please see me when you're ready," Ms. Renee calls across the room. She's returned to the front corner of the studio with Mr. Julian, and they're whispering heatedly. Heat lingers in Vivian's cheeks, knowing that they're surely discussing her audition and possible casting.

Which one of them does the final casting? Surely, Ms. Renee, right?

Vivian abandons her attempts at peeling off the tape, silicone toe protectors, and pointe shoe on her left foot in favor of clomping across the room half-barefoot.

When she limps up to the arguing pair, Mr. Julian snorts at her. It twists his face into something arrogant, and Vivian debates the likelihood of being cast if she throws her dead shoe at him.

Ms. Renee's eyebrows jump up, and she clicks her tongue at Vivian. "I said see me when you're ready." She points at Vivian's feet. "You don't look ready."

Vivian's cheeks heat. "I wasn't sure if there was anything else you'd like to see. I can throw my other shoe back on quickly if you want? Maybe another pass across the floor?"

The absolute last thing she wants to do is put her dead shoe back on. But if Ms. Renee wants to see another pass across the floor, Vivian will jeté across Studio B barefoot until her legs give out.

"That's not necessary. Thank you, Vivian."

Thank fucking god.

"We've been chatting"—Ms. Renee touches Mr. Julian's crossed forearm with something too close to affection—"and we'd like to offer you a role in the winter production."

Fuck yes! Fuckkkkkk, yesssss!

With every lingering spark of energy she has left, Vivian suppresses the urge to break into a huge, stupid grin. Ms. Renee isn't done speaking, and there's no telling what role they are offering. If they want to trick her into accepting some tiny role with one total minute of stage time, there is no benefit in showing her hand by celebrating too soon.

"Your hands are atrocious, and your jumps need work."

It's the first thing *he* has said to her since the parking lot. Since he insinuated that she was a homeless woman trespassing on private property. So much for her clothes conveying confidence and poise . . .

Mr. Julian continues, unaware or unconcerned by Vivian's inner rage, "You'll really need to put in *work* for this. Do you understand? You aren't going to be cast and then sneak by without putting in your hours."

Who is this guy?

"What part of my open audition, or even today, implies that I'm not willing to work?"

"—I wasn't finished," Mr. Julian interrupts. "Your fingers are stiff and unnatural; your jumps need work. But your turns were exquisite. What's your experience with pas de deux?"

Her turns were exquisite.

"Uhh—" Vivian stumbles, whiplash from his critiques and praise leaving her unbalanced.

What's the professional way to say that you've never performed pas de deux but that you're confident you could if given the chance?

He must be able to tell she's floundering because he interrupts again. "Never mind. I'll take care of it. You'll need to have reliable transportation for rehearsals. Can you manage that?" The way he slowly enunciates his words drips with disdain. Now, Vivian *really* wanted to throw her dead shoe at his head. Maybe it would knock some respect into him.

"Reliable" transportation.

Even after watching her dance—and complimenting her turns—this guy is concerned that she . . . What, stole a car or something? *Unbelievable.* Simply because she tumbled out of the back seat doesn't mean that her car is *unreliable.* Plenty of people have car issues. It's a perfectly normal occurrence. Unless he was somehow implying that she *lives* in her car?

Her studio apartment may be tiny and depressing, but it does have a working door handle at least.

Then, Ms. Renee jumps back in with the words that nearly stop Vivian's heart. "We'd like to cast you as a principal."

She goes on to explain something about rotating roles to avoid burnout and injury, how someone named Mr. Ben will be emailing her the rehearsal schedule, and when opening night falls in November, but Vivian's ears are still ringing.

We'd like to cast you as a principal.

The high of her new role keeps Vivian afloat even as she climbs over the center console of her car and slides into the driver's seat.

Chapter Five

Vivian meets with Maureen before rehearsal, one week after her initial audition. Despite the early hour, the sun is already out in full force. Vivian's home-made iced coffee is already sweating in the reusable cup she poured it into before rushing out of her studio. The condensation leaves a wet ring on the floor next to the chair she's taken in the conference room. When Maureen met her in the lobby, she'd mentioned something about renovations upstairs in the offices, and Vivian didn't bother to question her further.

"Sign here, initial here. I'll need your bank information for direct deposit as well as a photo ID. Did Ms. Renee discuss your salary and equipment stipend?"

Vivian's stomach drops, ice rushing through her veins in contrast with the August heat. Play it cool.

"Yes. We discussed it last week," she answers, carefully printing her bank account number on the designated line.

"Lovely," Maureen tuts, watching over Vivian as she writes.

"I'm afraid there's a small issue though."

Maureen flips through the paperwork, humming absentmindedly in response.

"I forgot my wallet at home this morning. I was nervous about my first day and . . ." Vivian trails off, trying to look as innocent and honest as possible. She's praying her appearance is as young and helpless as the nineteen-year-old she's pretending to be.

"Oh, I know what that's like. We try to be supportive, but this is a rigorous and demanding environment. I think a little intimidation might be healthy."

Well, that's a new take.

"Thank you for the advice," Vivian says demurely. "I appreciate it." She doesn't offer up another time to bring in her ID.

"Hmm. I'm not sure when I'm going to be back in the office," Maureen says, shuffling the paperwork around before guiding Vivian out of the conference room.

"I saw a flier with your office hours?" Vivian asks before she can think better of it. If Maureen doesn't care, she shouldn't be volunteering herself for trouble.

"Yes, well." Maureen clears her throat, and her gold necklaces swing when she gestures Vivian down the hall without making eye contact. "Since we're redoing the offices, I've been working from home lately. Remember to carry your wallet and I'll get a copy of your ID the next time I see you."

And then the older woman breezes down the hall without a backward glance. Vivian's stomach dips and swirls, recoiling with an innate sense of wrongness.

That was far too easy.

Part Two

The Adagio

Chapter Six

Kelsey Moore is a bitch.

It's a bold opinion for Vivian to adopt, given that they've only just met, but one meeting is more than enough to tell her everything she needs to know.

At her first company-wide rehearsal with Ellapond, Ms. Renee introduces her as their newest principal dancer. Vivian's near the cubbies in Studio A—the only rehearsal space large enough to hold the full company—twisting and angling her toe pads until they sit and cushion her toes just right. When she hears Ms. Renee clear her throat to introduce the newest members of Ellapond following the final round of casting for the season, she's quick to grab her shoes and stand. She doesn't want to meet a room full of cutthroat dancers sitting down and already in a place of spatial inferiority. Vivian is tying a sheer gray wrap skirt around her waist as she walks away from her cubby when a small brunette steps in front of her.

Well, the girl doesn't technically *step* in front of Vivian so much as she drops into a deep lunge and begins to stretch . . . right in Vivian's path. As if she hoped Vivian wouldn't see her and would *conveniently* happen to trip and fall on her way to being announced as Ellapond's new principal dancer. Her actions are neither subtle nor mature. When Vivian steps around her lunge, carefully avoiding the dangers posed by her outstretched limbs, the girl audibly huffs, as if disappointed that Vivian didn't fall for her obvious ploy.

But the lead weight in Vivian's stomach reminds her that while professional dancers face intense pressures and schedules, this girl could be as young as Vivian is pretending to be. As young as she's pretending to be. *How much maturity can you expect from a teenager?* This petite brunette with a dainty bun wearing a black leotard and baby pink skirt could be as young as fifteen. While Vivian might only be nine years older than her, watching the girl stretch makes her feel infinitely older. And far, *far* more jaded.

Ms. Renee claps her ring-studded hands before introducing Vivian, a lanky redheaded man—Alex Timmer, her fellow principal—and a smattering of other dancers littered around Studio A. Vivian sees the brunette visibly rolling her eyes. Then, Ms. Renee mentions that the young brunette—Kelsey Moore—is one of Ellapond's swings and Vivian watches as the sneer disappears behind a prim smile. *What a little faker.*

"As our swings, you can expect to see Kelsey, Derek, Marie, and Devonne at every rehearsal. Even the soloist- or principal-only rehearsals. Do your best to support them, as they're expected to learn the choreography for *all* roles."

The dancers each nod or wave in time with their respective introductions. The way Kelsey's fake smile drops into a glare from across Studio A screams that she's only interested in taking over one role: Vivian's. Vivian has no intention of supporting Kelsey in learning her role—or anything else. If Kelsey wants principal, she can pry it out of Vivian's cold, dead hands.

As Ms. Paige—Ms. Renee's assistant choreographer, a statuesque, umber-skinned woman with a severe bob and broad grin—leads a formal warm-up, the burden of her lies glues Vivian's feet to the floor. Each relevé is more difficult than the last.

Ms. Renee and Ms. Paige begin teaching the choreography of the opening number which features the corps, soloists, and principals. Vivian wishes she could revel in the joy of fresh choreography instead of wallowing in the distraction of her guilt.

"Glad to see you made it back," whispers the dark-haired dancer Vivian met at her company class audition.

Vivian shoots her a small smile as they mark Ms. Renee's choreography, a step behind her graceful movements.

"Glad to see you're still here," she shoots back.

"I'm Scarlett. Not sure if you remember from the company class." Vivian absolutely did *not* remember the other girl's name and is instantly grateful for the reminder. "I'm a soloist, so I'm not sure how much our schedules will overlap, but I'm happy to see a new face."

Scarlett's hair cascades down her back in a long braid. Her light blue leotard and complementary navy skirt appear new, but the scuffs and cuts on her pointe shoes mark her as a seasoned dancer. It's one thing to keep pristine shoes for performances but Vivian's never trusted a dancer whose rehearsal shoes don't look like they'd been a victim of assault. A quick glance across the room only heightens Vivian's building concern. Kelsey's shoes appear as though they're fresh out of the box, untouched.

"Thanks, Scarlett." Vivian commits the other girl's name to memory. "If you're looking for fresh blood, I'm happy to be of service."

They continue to whisper on the left edge of Studio A while Ms. Renee and Ms. Paige consult choreography notes in a spiral notebook that looks uncharacteristically worn for Ms. Renee's otherwise elegant persona.

"Have you met Alex or any of the other soloists yet?" Scarlett asks.

"I've met Ms. Renee, Mr. Julian, Ms. Paige, and now you. Oh, and Maureen!"

Scarlett flinches visibly. "Watch out for Maureen."

"Maureen in administration? *That* Maureen?"

Vivian has trouble imagining the woman who handles payroll and wears too many necklaces as a secret villain.

Scarlett nods somberly. "Yeah. How do you think they got Mr. Julian here? Ellapond is so new. They had to have some kind of pull or connections to get a dancer right off the circuit to teach. Or whatever they say he's doing." Scarlett wiggles her eyebrows while waving a dainty pale hand as though Vivian will understand the vague implication. She doesn't.

"He's right off the circuit? I assumed by artist-in-residence, they just meant that he was tired and taking time off from performing. Is he sticking around?"

She sneaks a glance around the room, only to find that he's noticeably absent from this *company-wide* rehearsal. How convenient.

Scarlett's dark braid whips over her shoulder as she eyes the surrounding dancers carefully. Whatever she knows must not be public knowledge.

"I don't really know much," she starts. "But there's just something *off*. Weird vibes. It seems like Maureen must have some kind of pull or something is happening behind the scenes. I think she's one of Ellapond's founders."

It's a well-known fact that dancers love to gossip. It's as much a part of ballet culture as pointe shoes and baby pink. But Scarlett's hushed words barely contain enough information to constitute gossip.

Vivian shrugs, unimpressed. "It's dance—someone always has connections."

Scarlett shakes her head, long braid swishing through the air. "It's extra connections then. Getting Mr. Julian right off the circuit to 'assist with duets?' And then there's you? No offense, but walking in off the street and getting principal? I'm glad you're here, but that doesn't mean it's normal."

Vivian's stomach churns with unease.

Before she moved to Brighton Harbor—which is neither bright nor anywhere near a body of water—with her parents in eighth grade, she'd never stepped foot in a dance studio. And using the word *studio* to describe the cramped, two-room dance school setup in the basement of a dental practice was generous.

All of Vivian's knowledge of the ballet world and its standard customs and conventions were doled out by Ms. Lorraine, the elderly Italian proprietor of Brighton Harbor Dance. While Ms. Lorraine was meticulous about pulling her bright red hair into neat buns and scolding Vivian every time she wore dead shoes during class, she had never imparted much wisdom about the internal structures or politics of dance studios. Vivian isn't naive enough to assume that casting and hiring don't involve a certain level of nepotism, but she's never had to contend with the idea as more than a hypothetical. Plus, she didn't know anyone before her audition and they cast her anyway. The weight of Scarlett's comments mixes with Vivian's guilt over her lies until nausea bubbles in her throat.

Scarlett nudges her with a sharp, graceful elbow. "You alright? I didn't mean to be rude."

Vivian shakes off the younger woman's apology quickly. "It's fine, I'm not upset. Just plotting to stay on Maureen's good side."

Scarlett nods at her sagely, as though Vivian's intent to avoid drama is the wisest choice she's ever made. The unease in her stomach still fizzes unpleasantly. What kind of issues would she even have with admin? It's *admin.*

"Alex was a soloist with me last season. I can introduce you during our lunch break. We usually head to the café around the corner if you want to join," Scarlett offers.

Vivian's stomach sinks notably lower at the reminder of her bank balance—not nearly as cushioned as she'd prefer for going out to lunch—but she slaps a smile on her face for Scarlett's benefit anyway.

"I'd love that."

Dancers are too ruthless for Vivian to turn down a genuine offer of friendship.

As they go across the floor to the echoing sounds of Ms. Renee's staccato claps, Vivian breathes through the guilt and anxiety in her stomach.

A new friend and the principal role with Ellapond Ballet Company are worth celebrating. Even if they came at the price of lies.

Chapter Seven

When they break for lunch, Alex is quick to seek out Scarlett, and consequently, Vivian. The girls are untying their skirts and slipping on pants and shoes—ratty, oversized sweatpants for Vivian and cropped leggings for Scarlett—when Alex finds them.

"Timmer, meet your new girl, Vivian," Scarlett introduces. Vivian raises an eyebrow.

"'Cause you'll be dancing together," Scarlett clarifies quickly. "As partners."

Vivian can't help but laugh at the younger girl's quick backtracking.

Alex is tall and lean with shaggy, disheveled strawberry-blond hair. Based on his baby face, lack of stubble, and slim build, Vivian would guess he's around Scarlett's age. His lips are curved into an easy smile when he bumps

Scarlett with his empty water bottle. He beams at Vivian and thrusts a lanky hand forward.

"Alex Timmer. I answer to either."

"Vivian Ladoe. I prefer Vivian."

While they chat through mouthfuls of overpriced but crisp salads and iced coffee, Vivian learns that Alex and Scarlett have known each other for years, even before Ellapond. Being only a year apart in age, they first met at *Relevé Dance Camp* in primary school and have shared a studio and stage countless times since then.

They steal off each other's plates as they talk, but there's an underlying tension when they discuss Ellapond that hints at rivalry bubbling below the surface.

As partners go, Vivian decides that she could be in much worse hands than Alex's—even if his grip does appear rather gangly.

"So, what do you make of Ellapond so far, Vivian?" Alex asks as he loudly slurps the last dredges of coffee from his cup.

"I'm so thankful to have been cast—"

Alex is quick to interrupt her carefully neutral response. "Sorry, I should've been more specific. What do you *honestly* think of Ellapond?"

He and Scarlett both lean in, as if suspecting Vivian will reveal some priceless gossip or impart the inspirational wisdom that landed her a principal role.

Vivian sips her iced coffee and clears her throat, stalling for an answer that will straddle the careful line between honesty and professionalism.

"Okay. Really?"

Alex and Scarlett nod so enthusiastically it's almost comical.

"I *am* really thrilled and thankful to have been cast. I know how rare it is to walk in off the street and get cast as principal. It almost seems . . . too good to be true, ya know? When I woke up for rehearsal, I kept expecting Maureen to call and tell me there'd been some misunderstanding. That I only needed to show up for company-wide rehearsals because I'd been demoted to corps."

Alex and Scarlett share a loaded stare that would have Vivian probing for answers if only she knew them for longer.

Alex shakes his empty cup, ice clinking loudly before leaning in and lowering his voice. "You should know what happened to our last principal."

Scarlett swats at Alex with her plastic forks, tines bending slightly where she flicks his bicep. "Stop making it sound like a ghost story." Scarlett turns to Vivian, eyeing her head-on. "It was weird but not ghost-story weird. Right before opening night—"

"I heard it was tech week," Alex interrupts.

"Oh, were you there?" Scarlett retorts, tossing her dark braid over her shoulder before swatting him again with her fork.

"Stop hitting me! And no, I wasn't there, but I heard from Kelsey—"

"Kelsey! Since when does she qualify as a reliable source of information?"

"Will you two stop bickering long enough to tell the story or what?" Vivian interrupts. "And should we be heading back soon? How strict are lunch breaks?"

"What time is it?" Scarlett asks, even as she's grabbing Alex's phone out of his hand to check the time.

"Shit! Ms. Renee is going to kill us if we bring her new star back late on the first day. Let's go, and I'll tell you the story on the way."

The three dancers scramble to clean their lunch trash from the tiny round table before hurrying out the door toward Ellapond.

As they're speed walking down the sidewalk, doing their best to hurry without sprinting, Scarlett says, "Basically, the last principal was injured right before opening night. Ms. Renee said she'd be out for a few weeks on medical, but then they recast the entire show last minute. They didn't even use the swings they'd already cast. The principal never came back, and I heard a few months ago from Kate that she was in the hospital. I don't know what happened, but Ms. Renee wouldn't say much."

Vivian shrugs wordlessly. Being cast as principal is a dream, one she keeps reveling in for fear that she'll wake up to find out it's all been a dream. No one talks about how a dancer's entire career relies on the integrity of the delicate tissues that support their joints—and their spins, leaps, jumps, and lifts. Ellapond's former principal dancer isn't the first to lose out on her career because of an injury, and she certainly won't be the last.

That's why Vivian plans to do everything within her power to guarantee her story ends differently.

Chapter Eight

The best part of being cast as principal by Ellapond is the joyous freedom that comes with dancing her heart out. The worst part is a tie between Kelsey and Mr. Julian.

Where Kelsey is immature and obvious in her dislike for Vivian as she tries to stand directly in front of her in every rehearsal, Mr. Julian's disdain is more subtle. It comes in the form of his indifferent gaze when she asks a question about choreography. Or his exasperated sighs when her arms don't float exactly the way he instructed. He's snippy, short, and all-around impatient.

It makes Vivian want to scream at him. It also makes her stay late after rehearsal, practicing in the hallway after hours or arriving early to give herself extra time to warm up. The opportunity to dance principal after walking off the street is practically unheard of, but she's willing to do whatever is necessary to keep her role. As much as she wants to throttle him for his attitude and countless snaps and comments of "Again," she also has a sneaking suspicion that by the time opening night rolls around in November, she'll be thanking him for pushing her so hard. It's a double-edged sword.

And she wants to wield it against Kelsey.

At every turn, the younger girl is trying to trip her up—figuratively and literally. She stands in Vivian's place if Vivian is even a moment late, as though no one will notice if she quietly slips into Vivian's role. She dances as close to Vivian as possible in rehearsals, mirroring her movements as if simply mimicking her will be enough to convince Ms. Renee to recast the performance. She catches Kelsey whispering with Marie, another of the swings, as they stretch and glare unsubtly at her.

If Kelsey's constant efforts to undermine her weren't frustrating enough, she seems to have some . . . connection with Mr. Julian. In her two weeks with Ellapond, Vivian's already come across the two several times, speaking in quick, hushed tones before rehearsal near the mirror or afterward in the hallway. Vivian wants to say that their behavior doesn't bother her—Who is she to care what they do in their free time?—but the churning in her stomach and the ache in her chest say otherwise. It's not obvious what exactly they're discussing, but the rushed whispers and private huddles point to something . . . untoward.

According to Scarlett, Kelsey is only seventeen. From the meticulous research Vivian did after her private audition, Mr. Julian is in his mid-thirties. It's not that Vivian wants to cast aspersions on the nature of their secretive whispers. The last thing she holds the moral ground on is someone's age but . . . *but, but, but.* Their whispers nag at her, similar to the gnawing sensation in her stomach when rehearsal goes late and she's run out of snacks.

Despite the frustration Kelsey inspires, fresh choreography, unlimited new pointe shoes, and the prestige of the principal role bloom as bright joy in Vivian's chest. She's never had a supply closet full of new shoes and tights. She's never had the spotlight.

Ellapond is simultaneously exhausting and invigorating. It's everything she dreamed of and far more than she bargained for.

Vivian's rehearsals are split between company-wide rehearsals, run by Ms. Renee, and principal duet rehearsals, run by Mr. Julian. Ms. Renee proves to be an austere and aloof instructor. She runs rehearsals from the front of the studio, elegantly perched on a stool or chair with a notebook, surely filled with elegant yet indecipherable notes. Every instruction from her is firm and measuring, as though she's judging Vivian on something as simple as the warm-up. Despite her sharp eyes that often bore into Vivian as she dances, it's rare that Ms. Renee makes any clear corrections. Instead, she prefers to *tut*, snap, clap, or simply shake her head when any movements aren't performed to her liking. Ms. Paige often serves to demonstrate new choreography to the studio, while Ms. Renee perches on her stool-throne, overseeing the room of her dancers akin to a queen eyeing unruly subjects. Ms. Renee's aloof demeanor only makes her beauty all the more intimidating. Her clothes are always neat and prim, with understated but expensive-looking jewelry. Her white-blonde hair alternates between a sharp ballet bun and a flawless blowout. Elegance and judgment cement her royal status within the studios of Ellapond.

In contrast to Ms. Renee's cool and calculating rehearsals, duet rehearsals with Alex and Mr. Julian are both invigorating and infuriating. With his slender frame, Alex makes for a graceful—but perhaps weak—partner. During most duet rehearsals, Vivian is shadowed by Kelsey, whose conniving attempts at tripping Vivian get notably more covert during these times. It's as if she desperately wants Vivian to lose her role, but she's smart enough to fall below Mr. Julian's notice. Unlike Ms. Renee's quiet judgments, Mr. Julian is vocal and direct with his criticisms.

"What was that? I said entrechat, not a hippopotamus learning to walk!"

"Slow, slow, slowwww. You're rushing."

"Are you listening at all, Sugar Plum? I said retiré, not cou-de-pied! Get that leg up."

"Let's go again."

"What are you guys doing? Again."

Mr. Julian stalks through Studio C, a jungle cat watching its pride. He examines them from every angle, quick to remind them, "You can do better than that."

Slightly over one week into Vivian's rehearsal schedule, she works up the courage to address him. They haven't spoken privately since their less than ideal parking lot meet-cute, and she's eager to dispel the lingering tension. Maybe if she clears the air, he'll stop eyeing her legs as if he's planning murder. She lingers by the barre as Alex and Kelsey pack up, stuffing shoes into their respective bags and digging out street clothes to wear home.

"Mr. Julian, do you have a minute?"

He peers at her from under the brim of his ball cap, dark curls peeking out over his ears. His eyes remind Vivian of spring rainstorms, bright golden sunbeams sparkling on damp fresh grass. His gaze is intoxicating. If Vivian didn't want to clear the air between them, she'd be tempted to continue staring into them as if she's a young girl with her first crush.

"Just Julian is fine."

"Okay, Just Julian," Vivian says, trying for a joke.

He doesn't laugh. So much for that.

"I wanted to clear the air after our . . . less than ideal meeting."

"You mean, after you fell out of a car in broad daylight? Were you drunk? Were you sleeping in your car?"

His expression is calm and neutral. Indignation bubbles up in Vivian all the same.

"I was neither drunk nor sleeping in my car! If you *must* know, the door handle broke off when I was getting in. So I had to use the backseat."

It's a perfectly reasonable explanation of a perfectly normal problem.

"The handle inside the car broke?"

"No, the handle of the driver's door on the outside."

"And so it didn't open from the inside?"

Oh. *Oh.*

Vivian is an idiot. But Mr. Julian—no, *Julian*—doesn't need to know that.

"Correct," she lies. "The driver's door isn't working correctly." There, that wasn't technically a lie.

Her first paycheck hasn't arrived from Ellapond yet. But once it does, everything not set aside for rent and groceries will go to buying enough duct tape to reattach the handle.

"Okay. Maybe get that fixed, Sugar Plum. Or don't. As long as you make it to rehearsal, I don't care how you get here," he says with a dismissive nod. His attention has strayed to something over her shoulder. Frustration burns in her belly and the nickname brings a heat to her cheeks. Vivian's embarrassed and improbably turned on. This isn't the professional reconciliation she intended.

"Yeah. That's not a problem. But I wanted to—"

"Mr. Julian, can I speak with you? *Privately*," a singsong voice interrupts.

Kelsey appears at Vivian's side, unraveling her chestnut hair from its bun. Her impossibly long and shiny mane falls over her shoulders, and she fluffs it while gazing up at Julian expectantly. She doesn't even glance at Vivian.

Julian stares at Vivian and his jaw tightens a tick. Vivian has no idea what it means. Is he annoyed by Kelsey's interruption, or is he irritated with Vivian for delaying them from another secretive chat?

"Are we done here, Ladoe."

He says the words flatly, making it clear that it's not a question, so Vivian nods.

"Yes. Thank you for your time, Mr. Julian."

He winces, then he turns to Kelsey without another word.

Chapter Nine

L e Pinson is an original production. The brainchild of Ms. Renee and Ms. Renee alone—or so she claims. The plan is for a twelve-performance run over the course of a month. Then the show will be scrapped, and Ellapond will start fresh, learning and preparing an entirely new performance, likely another Renee Dumont original.

Vivian's contract takes her through twelve weeks of rehearsal and four weeks of performing *Le Pinson*, with the option for renewal. Despite her lack of real-world experience with a professional company, from what Alex and Scarlett have indicated, it's a fairly typical timeline.

It still feels as though time is flying by. With no *real* experience on a stage other than the Brighton Harbor Community Center—a large but dated multipurpose venue used for everything from weddings to community fundraisers—each day that ticks her closer to *Le Pinson's* opening night is a paradox. Being onstage, especially front and center, is more than Vivian could have dreamed of when she moved to Bristol. It's also bone-achingly intimidating.

What if she falls? What if she messes up? What if she develops temporary insanity, forgets all her choreography, and Kelsey has to step in?

And her anxiety only burrows deeper into the space between her toes, the pit of her stomach, and the tension of her fascia when she remembers that she can hardly confide her fears in Scarlett. The younger girl likely assumes that Vivian's background is similar to her own—similar to Alex's, Kelsey's, Devonne's, and that of all the dancers at Ellapond. Years of tutus, tights, and buns starting as soon as they could stand. While Ellapond may be a newer studio, its dancers were born and bred to dance. It's in their bones.

And though it's in Vivian's bones too, she's spent most of her life only coveting the tools, teachers, and resources they've had at their fingertips. It leaves her with a desperate sense of determination that settles in her throat. Her performance—not only her performances but her rehearsals too—needs to be a show of skill and mastery. For some of the corps performers, dance is a passion. For Vivian, it needs to be a religion.

"Vivian." Ms. Renee's voice chimes down the echoing hall-way between studios.

Vivian almost drops her bag of clothes and gear at the sound. She's early to a duet rehearsal, mentally running through choreography while pacing as she waits for Alex to arrive. There's a swinging braid of dark hair behind her before Scarlett pops her head out of Studio B to wave at Vivian. Ms. Renee must be running a rehearsal for the soloists.

"Hi, Ms. Renee. Did you need me?"

The question sounds foolish in the wake of Ms. Renee's overwhelming presence. Her blonde hair is down, hanging in carefully crafted swoops and waves over her shoulders. She's wearing what appears to be a deep violet one-piece jumpsuit with severe creases pressed into the legs that only a woman with her height and poise could pull off. Vivian's certain that the same outfit would look like a purple potato sack on her.

"Can you go see Maureen? We need to get your mea-surements over to Costume. We take measurements every spring to ensure we keep the right sizing in stock, but since you only joined us recently, you're the only one missing measurements."

"I have rehearsal with Alex and Mr. Julian starting, but I can see her afterward. How late is she here?"

Ms. Renee scans Vivian up and down, as though attempting to intuit her sizes and measurements. "I suppose I could guess. You're not as tall as Scarlett, but you're curvier than Kelsey." The older woman hums, gaze fixed on the slight curve of Vivian's hips.

In twenty-four years, Vivian has not once been described as "curvy." With yellow-blonde hair, below-average height, and a slim build, Vivian's always felt closest to a pixie. Ms. Lorraine used to say she was "petite but packed a punch." Vivian is nothing close to the ample figure Ms. Renee seems to be implying with her words and gaze. If Ms. Renee thinks she's "curvy," Vivian is worried what the other woman would guess her measurements to be.

"That's okay. I can just go see Maureen after rehearsal. How late did you say she's here?"

It's a well-known fact that Maureen keeps no schedule other than her own. When Vivian tried to track her down to make sure that she'd supplied all the information necessary to set up direct deposit, the other woman was nowhere to be found despite the office hours clearly posted on her office door that indicated she was meant to be *in her office*. After asking Scarlett, Vivian learned that Maureen is notoriously difficult to track down in person but infallibly reliable to reach via email.

"I think she's leaving soon. You should *really* go see her now," Ms. Renee insists.

Warmth tickles the back of Vivian's neck only a tenth of a second before she hears Mr. Julian's—no, *Julian's*—voice from above her.

"Ms. Ladoe has rehearsal now, Renee. What do you need with her?" He speaks right over Vivian, as though she's in another room instead of standing right in front of (and below) him. It's unbearably condescending.

She wonders if Ms. Renee would notice if she kicked him. It's probably best not to chance it. She's not sure she'd survive him kicking her back.

"Maureen needs to see her for measurements," Ms. Renee informs him primly.

Vivian senses a hint of disdain in their interaction, and she glances at Julian to see if it's two-sided. As usual, he's frowning slightly, an expression that could indicate anything from rage to mild heartburn. If pressed, Vivian would admit that he has the most attractive resting bitch face she's ever seen.

"And Maureen needs to see her *now*? Right as I'm beginning rehearsal?" Mr. Julian asks.

Ms. Renee lifts one shoulder and flits her hand through the air, a vague and airy gesture. It's as though Vivian's instructors are holding two simultaneous conversations, one through direct and simple words, and another—far more complex—through their gestures and body language. Not for the first time, the question of their history pings through Vivian's mind as a warning bell. Whatever the source of their tension is, she's not interested in getting in the middle of it.

She interrupts, ready to leave the minefield of the hallway where these two are staring each other down.

"I can see Maureen quickly, and I'll be back for rehearsal before you even know I'm gone. I already warmed up, but Alex only just arrived"—she desperately points at where he's talking to Scarlett outside the doors to Studio B—"and he'll need to warm up. I'll be done with Maureen by the time he's ready." Vivian hasn't seen Kelsey arrive, and she's not going to offer up the younger girl to fill in for her. That seems far too close to tempting fate.

Mr. Julian hums and turns, leaving through the doors to Studio C without another word.

Okay then.

Chapter Ten

Maureen Patino's office is on the second floor, through one of the four doors in a dimly lit hallway. Vivian's never had reason to come up to the second floor, with all the studios, the conference room, and the main supply room conveniently located on the ground floor. After passing Ms. Renee's office, the shared office that Ms. Paige and Mr. Ben share, and a third office with a piece of paper conspicuously taped over the metal placard on the door where a name should be, she finds Maureen's office.

Vivian knocks on the cracked door, before entering to the older woman's distracted hum.

"Ladoe, finally!"

Vivian's never particularly enjoyed being called by her last name, but from the harried way Maureen's hand is waving a full mug of coffee through the air, maybe now isn't the time to take a stance.

There's a shorter woman with a choppy dark bob and a deep olive complexion standing right behind Maureen. The two women are studying something on Maureen's computer screen with pursed lips and critical eyes.

"Ms. Renee said you needed my measurements?" Vivian prompts when neither woman moves their attention from the computer. There's an impatient Julian waiting for her downstairs and despite what she implied, there's only so long that Alex can stall by stretching. If Vivian returns to rehearsal to find that Kelsey has *stepped in*, she might contemplate homicide.

"We'll be with you in a minute," Maureen says dismissively before pointing a manicured fingernail to something on the screen.

Vivian drops into the stiff wooden chair across from Maureen's desk to wait.

"I don't know what they were thinking with these leotards," Maureen says to the other woman. "The sheer panels show off her love handles."

The other woman nods, her dark hair swishing along her jaw. "Ughh. And the neckline is obscene. Is this ballet or burlesque?"

"I expected better from Mouveaux. Their dancers look like elephants in tutus. Disgusting."

The two older women continue to critique the images on Maureen's computer, finding fault in every aspect of the costume and dancers. Vivian shifts uncomfortably in her seat, tension prickling her skin. Julian and Alex must be waiting on her by now, and these women are still picking at the images akin to bloodthirsty vultures scavenging roadkill.

Finally, Maureen slips her glasses off her nose, glasses chain instantly tangling with her multitude of necklaces.

"Let's get these measurements taken already, Ladoe." Maureen clicks her tongue impatiently, as if she's been waiting on Vivian instead of the opposite.

She bites back the indignation that wants to bubble out of her. Rehearsal is currently happening *without* her, and the last thing she needs is Kelsey getting too comfortable in her role.

"Great!" she says with overexaggerated enthusiasm. "Where do you want me?"

Maureen introduces the woman with the neat bob as Adelina, Ellapond's in-house Costume Mistress. The two women direct Vivian to a corner of Maureen's office where a full-length mirror hangs conspicuously. With some fiddling from Maureen with a set of switches next to the mirror, the corner is suddenly lit by a blinding fluorescent lamp along with a white-blue glow emitted directly from the mirror. The lamp sits to Vivian's left, perpendicular to the mirror. *Why do they even need a mirror for measurements?* If Vivian was taking her own measurements, that would be one thing, but with both Adelina and Maureen present, the mirror is entirely unnecessary.

"We'll begin with your inseam," Adelina says, whipping out a cloth measuring tape like a stage magician. It snaps in the air with a flick of her wrist.

With firm hands on Vivian's shoulders, Adelina positions her directly in front of the mirror, adjusting Vivian's posture until she's satisfied. The older woman bends, fingernails scraping carelessly at Vivian's inner thigh and ankle, and she measures Vivian's inseam.

"Twenty-nine," she says to Maureen, who's poised with a small notebook behind Vivian.

"A little on the short side," Maureen chides, as if Vivian is singularly and intentionally responsible for her petite stature.

Ignoring the older women who are managing to tread the line between talking *about* her and talking *to* her, Vivian tries to catch Maureen's eyes in the mirror.

"Do you happen to have my onboarding paperwork handy? I'm worried that I wrote down my bank information incorrectly."

"You wrote your information down wrong?" Maureen squawks.

"Well, no. I don't think so, but it's just that I haven't seen a deposit yet, and it's been a month and . . . "

"Girth next," Adelina interrupts, slipping her tape measure between Vivian's legs and up her torso to meet at the top of her right shoulder. Based on the placement of the lamp, Vivian's right shoulder is shrouded in shadow. *Can Adelina even read the tape?*

"Oh yes, that," Maureen says with a hand wave. "The accountant called and said something about verifying the routing number since it wasn't a local bank. I'm taking care of it. Be patient and we will work it out." She waves a hand, as if Vivian missing a month's worth of paychecks is a mild inconvenience that simply slipped her mind.

"Well, I could *really* use those paychecks for . . ."

"I'm taking care of it. I'll call the bank when we're done here," she snaps, her patience wearing thin.

Adelina tuts another number at Maureen, and Vivian mentally checks out, intentionally reviewing choreography in her head instead of listening to the other women. It isn't until Adelina gets to her waist that Vivian is forced back to reality.

"When we're done here, I'll email over your meal plan. If you start on it today, you'll be able to fit into your leotard in seven weeks," Maureen says.

"Sorry, what?" Vivian turns to peek at Maureen and makes the mistake of glancing to her left. Her eyes immediately well with tears when she catches sight of the blazing lamp. The intensity of light is blindingly sharp—intelligence agencies could use it for interrogations.

"You'll have to start right away if you want to get down to a twenty-four," Maureen reiterates with a huff. As though Vivian's confusion is more offensive than her implication that Vivian needs a meal plan.

"Why would I want to get down to a twenty-four?" Vivian asks. At 5'3", she's on the shorter side for a ballerina, and she knows the rest of her body is proportional to her height. With strong and lean but small limbs, she's in excellent shape for her chosen career—no meal plan needed.

Adelina scoffs, an airy sound escaping her from where she's bent next to Vivian's right hip. She stands, measuring tape snapping through the air again, leveling Vivian with an insincere smile.

"Principal with Ellapond is a *very* coveted role. A very . . . *demanding* role," Maureen says haughtily.

Adelina adds, "Surely, you want to do whatever is necessary to retain that role. Don't you?"

The older women stand right behind Vivian. With the strange lighting and dramatic mirror, it's all too easy to imagine them as miniature devils hovering over each of her shoulders.

The weight of their appraising eyes is heavy. They've taken stock of her and found her wanting.

"I'd appreciate you using my current measurements for all costumes," Vivian says, pouring as much energy as possible into keeping her voice neutral and even.

"Fine."

There's a distinct scratch of pen on paper, as though a number is being violently and repeatedly crossed out. One of the women huffs, but Vivian doesn't stick around long enough to find out which.

She escapes down the hallway of offices, pausing next to the door with paper taped over the nameplate. She leans a shoulder against the door, staring at the covered nameplate and wondering why they didn't simply change the name when they renovated the offices back in August. Her chest heaves as she gulps in oxygen as though she's been running.

Between the heavy-handed implication that she needs to lose weight and the complete disregard of her missing paychecks, anxiety and dread pulse through her veins.

The dozen or so steps she took to escape the clutches of Maureen and Adelina felt harder than running underwater, as though the hallway's air contained additional resistance. Suddenly, escaping downstairs to the reliable scrutiny of Julian's instruction is a welcome reprieve.

Part Three

Variation One

Chapter Eleven

With a sickening noise and a broken scream, disaster rains down on a Thursday afternoon.

It starts with an overhead lift that Julian has been drilling into them for what feels like years. Despite countless repetitions, Alex and Vivian still look "worse than dying fish wriggling for water," according to Julian.

Rehearsal began hours ago. They paused for lunch almost an hour ago and despite the respite, Vivian doesn't feel particularly rejuvenated. Alex's strawberry-blond curls are in a matted, sweaty disarray, and Vivian doesn't appear much better. She can hear Julian click his tongue or adjust his hat whenever she tightens her ponytail or fixes her leotard. Easy for him to complain when he's lounging in the corner and snapping at them with long, impatient fingers. He's easily the hottest drill sergeant Vivian has ever met.

Kelsey has been restricted to the corner of Studio C after Julian saw her almost trip Vivian while shadowing her too closely. He placated the younger girl with the promise that she would get to practice the lifts with Alex once he and Vivian had a few more tries. Vivian can practically hear her fuming with rage. At least she won't trip on Kelsey now, even if she may fall victim to the other girl's glares later.

"One last time. Sugar Plum, you need to keep your core tight when Timmer rolls you down. No more floppy fish!" Julian barks.

Vivian can't repress the eye roll. It's practically instinct. "We're not even doing *The Nutcracker*. I'm not the Sugar Plum Fairy," she grumbles under her breath.

"What was that, Sugar Plum? You want to go from the top again?" The devilish smirk on Julian's face says that he knows *exactly* what she mumbled.

"No, Mr. Julian. From the glissade is fine with me," she responds quickly. Vivian has absolutely no interest in going from the top.

"Alright. From the glissade and *stay tight* when you roll," Julian reiterates. "Ready, Timmer?"

Alex's flushed and fatigued head nods, and Vivian prepares for Julian's snapping fingers to count them in.

5, 6, 7, 8.

Vivian glides across the hardwood, limbs heavy with fatigue. Her serene ballerina face is long gone, replaced with a sharp grimace of determination and pain. She's never trained this way before. Partner work is new to her and partner lifts while tired down to the bone is an even scarier beast.

The instant her knees bend and her feet extend to push her body off the ground—the very instant she leaves the floor—she knows the lift is off. Her body is hardening concrete, fighting a losing battle against gravity. Alex's hands are clammy when they catch her body, fingers digging into sensitive tissue when he times the catch too late.

When he presses her up, heaving her weight above his head with an effortful huff, she thinks they've pulled it off. It isn't pretty, but it isn't a catastrophe. They executed the lift, at least. Vivian tightens her core and extends her leg as Alex holds her above him. They're both trembling with the effort and Vivian knows Julian can see it from his stool. After a beat that might have lasted a century, she initiates the dismount, tucking her chest toward Alex's so she can roll down his body.

And then it happens.

Inexplicably, the *before* happens so slowly that she can feel every molecule, every atom, of her body that Alex's sweaty grip is no longer holding. He *isn't* holding her. Her body plummets freely toward the hardwood.

Then her perception catches up with reality to form *now*. Alex's fingers catch and tighten on her bicep, slowing her perilous descent. But her body misses the memo and continues to fall while her arm stays right where it's gripped by his slick fingers.

There's an audible *pop.* Then nauseating pain and a pervasive sensation of wrongness.

Alex lowers her to the floor, still tightly clutching her throbbing arm. He follows her down to kneel next to her. Vivian thinks he's saying something—hopefully, an apology for his terrible grip—but she's preoccupied with the limp dangle of her right arm. Julian is yelling—maybe at Alex or even her—but the pain and shock are overriding everything else.

Fuck.

Then Julian is next to her, careful fingers cool on her wrist.

"You're okay, sweetheart. Let me see," he whispers from near her hair.

Vivian cradles her arm against her chest, instinctively protective of the injury. In the time that can only be titled *after*, Julian inspects her hand, wrist, forearm, and as much of her bicep and shoulder as she'll allow.

"I don't think you broke anything, but we'll need an ER trip for X-rays and to get your shoulder reset," he says while helping her from her heap on the floor.

Julian's hands are noticeably less clammy than Alex's, and she doesn't mind when he settles one on her back to usher her through the studio toward the exit. Kelsey comes to stand near the doorway, a maniacal gleam in her eye. Vivian knows that Kelsey wasn't involved in the fall at all—no, Alex gets *all* the credit for this one—but she can't help wondering if Kelsey threw together a quick voodoo doll while she was sulking.

"Timmer, Moore, go home. I'll be in touch." Julian's voice is rougher than she remembers ever hearing. And she's heard him yell many times over the past three weeks.

"Wait, I need my stuff," Vivian interrupts. "And honestly, I can take myself to the ER. It's only a dislocated shoulder."

Zaps of electric pain and a wrongness that manifest as a churning nausea plague her, even as she tries to downplay the injury. But stabs and nausea aside, her pain isn't *that* bad. *It can't be that bad.*

She's never dislocated a joint before. Vivian has no idea whether that's her only injury, but pain and shock are sending millions of pins and needles through her body. Then there are also the consequences of her injury to worry about. How many rehearsals will she have to miss? What if it's not just a dislocation? What if there's soft tissue damage? *What if . . . ?* Anxiety heightens the dancing electric current in her limp arm and veins. She doesn't need a chaperone or a chauffeur to the hospital. She'd prefer not to be within three square miles of Julian when her tears start falling.

Julian simply hefts her bag onto his shoulder and continues urging her toward the parking lot.

"Nice try, Sugar Plum, but I'm required to ensure my dancers receive adequate and timely medical attention when they're under my care."

My dancers, under my care, and *Sugar Plum* bounce through Vivian's addled brain until they've warped into a nonsensical chant that fills her head for the duration of the ride to Saltland County Regional Hospital.

Chapter Twelve

Julian rolls his eyes when he finds Vivian in a curtained-off bed in the furthest corner of the ER, attempting to wedge a hospital clipboard between her hip and the forearm of her injured arm. His hat is pulled down low over his eyes, curls appearing especially disheveled, and he's spinning his car keys around one finger lazily. Even in the unforgiving fluorescents of a hospital, he's alluring.

"What are you doing. You look absurd." It's not phrased as a question. Has he ever asked a question before? Vivian can only imagine what it must be like to navigate the world with such surety.

"You already parked? They said they need intake information. If I balance this, I think I can scribble with my other hand."

Vivian does her best to gesture at the clipboard without extending her right arm.

Julian plucks the paperwork from her grip before she manages to mangle it or herself further.

"Give me the pen too."

"Thanks for the ride, but you don't have to stay. I can get Scarlett to pick me up. I'm not sure how long this will take."

Her arm is somehow throbbing and tingling simultaneously, her fingers are a worrisome shade of mauve, and the last thing she can handle is a cranky Julian King intimidating nurses.

Julian ignores her and begins filling in her intake form.

He scrawls her first and last name down before pausing. "Middle initial?"

"C."

"Catherine?"

"No. Celeste."

"Vivian Celeste?" Julian raises an eyebrow but doesn't inquire further. "Birth date?"

Maybe it's the pain in her shoulder and arm, maybe it's the fear that's eating away at her carefully constructed lies, maybe it's something else entirely. Regardless, Vivian rattles off her birthday without a second thought.

Her *real* birthday.

Every atom of Julian stills, pen still hovering just above the paper.

He's frozen, and Vivian is absolutely certain that all of her hopes of a professional ballet career have died a miserable death with this truth.

Fuck.

"How old are you."

In any other voice, on any other day, the sentence would be a question, but Julian spits the words as if they hurt to speak. As if their very existence pains him. God knows, it hurts Vivian to hear them. It hurts that she's watching her dream career fade away in real time, and it hurts that he's going to be the one to take it away.

Her shoulder hurts, her hand hurts, and now her heart hurts. So she says the first stupid thing that comes to mind.

"Well, I was born on Leap Day. And it only happens every few years, you know? So the other ones don't count."

It has to be the dumbest thing that has ever come out of her mouth. Without a doubt. They both know it. Her secret is out, and there's no going back now, even as she's desperately scrambling for a handhold below the cliff she's thrown herself off.

"You are the worst liar I've ever seen."

Vivian can't decide if Julian looks enraged or broken. There's a tic in his jaw and a tightening around his eyes that make Vivian's stomach churn like a washing machine set to the extra spin cycle. His expression is indescribable. She never wants to see him this way again, and yet she can't stop staring.

"I can explain—"

That's when the radiology tech wanders in, rolling equipment with her and appearing decidedly unimpressed with Vivian. Monica snaps her gum and pulls on a pair of blue gloves like she's ready to play Operation.

"You said you hurt your shoulder *dancing*?"

Monica verifies Vivian's intake paperwork, positions her body with painfully apathetic gloved hands, and confirms that the X-rays show exactly what Vivian already knew. Her right shoulder is dislocated.

Monica snaps her gum again. Should she even be chewing that around patients?

"I'm gonna grab your doc, and then we'll pop that thing right back in," she says, gesturing at Vivian's limp arm. "Then you two can get back to *dancing*."

Monica raises a skeptical eyebrow in time with her words before flouncing away. The moment she's past the curtain, Vivian's spinning toward Julian.

"If you can just let me explain—or maybe you should leave?"

Vivian is torn between the desperate pull to keep Julian in sight where she knows he isn't calling Ms. Renee and getting as far away from him and his broken expression as she can. Should she send him away and hope he'll stay quiet or continue suffering through his silent brooding? The choice feels impossible.

Julian pulls his hat off and runs a hand over his face and into his hair, pulling a little. His brown curls under the hat are rumpled and lopsided, slightly favoring the right side of his head. He sighs, spins the hat to settle it back on backward, and Vivian's stomach drops. It feels far closer to the swing of the gallows than the turning of a baseball cap. How can a simple gesture be so ominous?

"Let's deal with your shoulder first, Ladoe."

Ladoe. Fucking *Ladoe?*

He never calls her by her last name.

He's sitting in an ugly, plastic orange hospital chair merely six feet away from where she sits on the exam table, but Vivian swears an ocean would fit between them. She hates the empty, panging ache that settles in her stomach.

He knows she lied. He knows she lied about her age so Ellapond would cast her. So that *he* would work with her. He knows she lied, and he's simply sitting there, waiting for some faceless doctor to shove her shoulder back where it belongs after Alex dropped her. He *knows* her secret, and she has no idea what happens now.

It turns out that what happens next is "closed reduction." At least, those are the words Vivian catches the ER doctor mumbling as he snaps gloves on and reaches for her limp arm.

"Monica already gave you something for the pain, right?" the doctor asks without even glancing up from where he's examining her shoulder.

"Uhh, yeah. But I think it was only—"Vivian's voice cuts out when the ER doctor lifts her right wrist away from where she has been protectively cradling it against her torso.

Ibuprofen.

All Monica gave her was fucking ibuprofen. Is that supposed to count as something for the pain? From the panic soaring through her veins at the doctor's minimal movement of her arm, ibuprofen isn't sufficient in the least. It's not doing nearly enough to manage her pain—or her newfound panic.

But he hasn't bothered to hear what exactly Monica gave her; Vivian's assent is sufficient. He continues on, "I'm going to rotate your arm, and we'll see if that shoulder can slip right back in."

"And if it doesn't?" Vivian's never dislocated her shoulder before. Hell, she's never dislocated anything before. She's suffered her share of bumps, bruises, rolled ankles, sore muscles, scrapes, and cuts. But never a dislocation. Do shoulders *slip in and out* the way the doctor's implying? That doesn't sound safe.

"If we can't maneuver it back, we'll have to consider applying pressure or more imaging."

Vivian isn't interested in more imaging. She wants to get out of this hospital and back to rehearsal. She sure as hell doesn't want to find out what "applying pressure" means.

"Yeah, okay," she mumbles.

Despite agreeing to the closed reduction, Vivian finds that everyone in the tiny, curtained area of the ER is simply staring at her. Monica, the ER doctor, and even Julian, are closely watching her.

"What? Let's do it already. I have to get back to rehearsal." She's getting impatient. *Shouldn't the magical ibuprofen have kicked in by now?*

"We're going to need to talk about rehearsal—" the doctor says.

Julian is quick to cut him off. "You have to give him your arm, Sugar Plum. He can't fix it if you won't let him touch it."

Vivian didn't realize, but in the time that the doctor was telling her about imaging and pressure, she'd managed to pull her legs up onto the exam table, propping her injured arm between her chest and bent knees. Her bent legs form a protective cradle, and she's curved her entire body around her injured arm without noticing. Her shoulder and arm are still throbbing despite Monica's pitiful ibuprofen, Julian knows she lied to Ellapond about her age, and now she's supposed to hand her injured shoulder over to this doctor for whatever the hell a "closed reduction" is?

Nope. No, thank you.

Tears well in the corners of her eyes, and a tickle ricochets in her throat. Vivian sniffles, staring vacantly down at her arm. *This is the most embarrassing moment to get emotional.*

She hears the soft rumble of Julian's voice asking, "Can we have a minute?" before the flimsy curtain around the exam table is opened and re-closed. The fastenings of the curtain *clang* together sharply.

Warm, strong fingers wrap around her ankles and tug them gently away from the tight ball she's made of her body.

"You're fine. It's only a dislocation. There's no fracture and you'll only need a sling for a few days." Julian notably *does not* mention Ellapond or rehearsal. "But the longer it's out of place, the tighter and angrier your muscles and tissues are getting. You know that inflammation makes everything worse. You need to let him put it back."

"What about . . ."

She can't say it. It's one thing for Julian to have discovered her lie, but it's another thing entirely for her to admit it aloud. Again.

"We'll talk about it later." His expression is neutral and impenetrable.

Vivian wants to scream. She wants to cry and scream and throw a tantrum like the child he thinks—*thought*—she is. It's not fair that Alex dropped her, and it's not fair that she had to lie about her age just to get on that stage. It's not fair that now that her dreams are within her grasp, Julian, of all fucking people, will be the one to rip them from her. Not Ms. Renee, who could tell her that she's just not good enough. Not Kelsey, who's been working toward a principal role since she could walk. Not any of the assistant choreographers or Ellapond employees. No, it's *him*. Him and his stupid hat, demanding rehearsals, beautiful jawline, and effortless grace.

If he's not going to give away his next move, then neither is she.

"Fine, get the doctor back in here."

He doesn't move though. His warm hands are still branding her ankles.

"You gonna need me to hold your hand, Sugar Plum?"

Vivian scoffs, desperately wishing she could agree. *Yes, please hold my hand or my ankle. Hold anything you want.*

"Get the doctor back in here before I fix this damn arm myself."

It's all bluster, and she knows that he knows it too when he snorts before pulling open the curtain.

Chapter Thirteen

The mood in the car is silent but awkward as Julian drives her home in the flashy sports car from the day they first met. Her shoulder is sore but hurting significantly less now that it's back where it belongs.

But instead of driving back to Ellapond so Vivian can pick up her car, Julian turns left and heads downtown.

"You'll need to tell me when to turn."

She absolutely does not want to tell him when to turn. Vivian has no interest in bringing Julian anywhere near her shoebox of an apartment.

"Just take me back to the studio. I have to get my car anyway."

He scoffs without looking at her. "You're supposed to rest your arm."

"I don't need two hands to drive, but I do need my car to get to rehearsal tomorrow."

Julian scoffs again like an arrogant idiot. "What makes you think you're rehearsing tomorrow?"

Vivian's stomach sinks. Her shoulder aches, she's painfully tired, and now he's going to have her kicked out of Ellapond? Intellectually, it makes sense that she used up all of her body's adrenaline after the fall, injury, and subsequent birth date revelation. It makes sense that she's crashing now. Somehow, that knowledge still isn't enough to stop the tears welling or the burning of her cheeks.

"That's not fair. I know I lied, but I can explain. Let me talk to Ms. Renee. You don't have to get me fired."

The car jolts slightly as Julian pulls over suddenly, double-parking on a side road next to an ugly red minivan.

"I'm not firing you, Sugar Plum. You just dislocated your shoulder. You can't rehearse tomorrow. You need rest."

Rest?

She's not convinced so she keeps silent, waiting for the other shoe to drop.

"I'm not going to tell Renee. Not now, anyway. But you need to take some time off. At least a week, and that ER doctor recommended even longer. You'll need to ease back into it too. Don't make me use Kelsey for opening night. Her pirouettes are atrocious."

Vivian laughs, but it sounds closer to a sob.

"Fuck Kelsey."

Julian shakes his head, refusing to agree, but Vivian desperately hopes he shares in the sentiment. Despite their strange, whispered meetings, he agreed—or at least didn't vocally disagree—with Ms. Renee's choice to cast Vivian as principal. Not Kelsey. That has to mean *something*.

She can't help but ask. The question that has been burning a hole in her mind, in her heart, since the words first fell from him, tossed by the barre like scraps of sweetness for her to chase after.

"Why 'Sugar Plum?'"

He pulls his hat off, runs a hand roughly through his hair, and then returns the hat to its backward throne atop his curls. Even through Vivian's tears, he looks stupidly sexy.

"I'm only going to say this once, and then we're never going to talk about it again." He drums on the steering wheel, refusing to meet her teary-eyed gaze. Dread accumulates as a tsunami, building until it towers impossibly high above. An impenetrable wall of water, waiting to crash down and drown her. Vivian remains silent, trying not to sniffle too audibly.

"All this time—Fuck. All this time, I've been hating myself and trying to hate you. I thought there was something wrong with me. I thought I was sick for lusting after a fucking child. There was no way—you have to understand that I would *never*—" He breaks off, gaze still fixed on the steering wheel.

"The Sugar Plum Fairy is joy. She's compassion, confection, and—most importantly—out of reach. She's childhood dreams and unattainable goals. During your audition, you landed your pirouettes as if you danced on a cloud. As if gravity was your champion, eagerly bending to your will. Fuck, Vivian, you showed up to the *YA* company class. What do you want me to say? You could've been fifteen!"

The veins in his hands surge as he strangles the leather steering wheel. It's stupid that even his hands are hot. The fantasy of those long, deft fingers curling around her instead of the steering wheel is too tempting to ignore.

Vivian's heart does its best to jump out of her chest and into his hands.

All this time? All this fucking time, he's been nothing but rude to her because he wanted her but thought she was too young for him?!

"You're an idiot. And an asshole."

When he finally, *finally* meets her gaze, the tightening around his hazel eyes resembles anguish rather than anger. Frustration burns in the back of her throat.

"I don't care how old you thought I was, that's no reason to be cruel. You're the 'adult' here—act like it."

Tears still stream down her cheeks, but now they're boiling from her frustration instead of fear. Whoever designed her body to cry when faced with heightened emotion needs to cut her some slack.

"Who cares how old I am if I can fill the seats?"

"You obviously care, or you wouldn't have lied."

"I *don't* care. I might have lied to Ellapond, but I'm not lying to myself."

"Aren't you?"

"No."

Julian sighs, weighty and weary. "Well, that makes one of us."

He navigates the car back onto the road and drives her home.

They don't speak of it again, any of it. Not her lie, not his admission, not her sling, or even her car that's sitting alone in Ellapond's parking lot.

The only break in the silence comes when Vivian directs him to an apartment complex four blocks away from her own. It's close enough to her real address to be believable but in notably better condition than her actual studio. She gets lucky and manages to slip into the lobby behind another resident—a real resident—when Julian insists on waiting until she's inside before driving off. She nods at him from the lobby and waits until three minutes have passed after he drives off before she ducks back out of the building.

It's raining lightly when she emerges from 1005 Custrel Complex and makes the five-minute walk to her real apartment on Glenmarie Street. Rain seeps into the thinning canvas of her dance bag and clings to her limp hair.

When Vivian collapses onto the lumpy, pea-green futon that serves as both her bed and couch, silence lingers, a gray cloud of emotion she can't bring herself to clear away.

Chapter Fourteen

Since her first steps into Brighton Harbor Dance, dance has always been Vivian's. It has belonged to her in a way that very little else in her life has. She has always had something that the other dancers—with their countless leotards in every color and seemingly infinite supply of shoes—lacked.

Vivian's always had a lack of respect for moderation.

She doesn't do anything by halves, wouldn't know how to if she tried. It's impossible not to *want* and *try* with every molecule of her body. Every point of her foot uses her complete range of motion. Every leap gets the fullest extension and then a little more. Utilizing every ounce of her energy, body, and ability is the only way she knows how to dance. It's the only way worth dancing. Since the evenings after school she spent helping Ms. Lorraine with data entry and cleaning the studio in order to pay for her classes, she's always given everything. It's bittersweet to think that dedication has brought her all the way to Ellapond. To Ms. Renee, Scarlett, Kelsey, and Alex. To Julian. To the dull throb in her shoulder and the sharp stabbing in her heart. To these overwhelming emotions of anxiety and frustration.

In her—admittedly brief—dance career, Vivian has never suffered an injury severe enough to push her onto the sidelines. She's danced on rolled ankles, bruised toes, and other minor injuries. Even when she broke her finger after closing a car door on it, Ms. Lorraine just eyed her finger skeptically and asked if the splint could be color-coordinated with her skirt. Vivian's never been forced to stop dancing before, and the stakes have never been this high before.

What are all the lies, work, and time for if her career is over before it began? From her lies to Ms. Renee, Maureen, and everyone at Ellapond, her move to Bristol, her tolerance of Kelsey, her patience with Alex's sweaty hands . . .

She's put in so much work only to have her dream crash and burn before it even gained traction.

Scarlett:

> Alex told me what happened. How are you feeling?

Scarlett:

> It's okay if you're mad at him but he feels really bad.

Smoothies later? I'll pick you up so you don't have to drive with a sling.

The chattering of her phone vibrating against the un-even multipurpose wooden table—her coffee table, book-case, dining table, and nightstand—pulls Vivian from her wallowing. When the buzzing persists, she answers the incoming call without bothering to glance at the screen.

"Thanks for the offer, Scarlett, but I'm not really in the mood. I'm exhausted. Tell Alex—"

"Tell Timmer what?" a deeper voice asks.

"Hello?" she asks in a wobbly voice. Vivian pulls the phone away from her face to see that the incoming num-ber isn't saved as a contact.

Then Julian's smooth voice melts through the air into her waiting ears. "Hey, Sugar Plum. Come outside."

Vivian's heart drops into her stomach as anxiety pulses through her veins. *Come outside?*

"What?"

"Did you suffer a head injury besides the shoulder dis-location, or are you simply not listening to me? Come outside. I brought your car. You'll have to drive me back though."

He brought her car. Here. To her studio apartment that's small enough to serve as a life-size dollhouse.

"You brought my car here? I'll be right down to drive you back." Maybe if she's fast enough, she can drive him right back to Ellapond without having to give him a tour.

"Sounds good. I'm in the lobby."

Four words shouldn't be enough to break a heart, but the fissure in her chest stabs her all the same when they register.

He's in the lobby.

Her apartment building on Glenmarie Street doesn't have a lobby. She's never made enough in her whole life to live somewhere with a *lobby*. But 1005 Custrel Complex—the building she ducked into last night—sure does.

"You there?" Julian's voice lowers until he's whispering into the phone. "There's a lady with an orange cat on a leash eyeing me. Can you come down already?" Despite the words, his deep timbre leaves Vivian's arms covered in goosebumps.

"Who's eyeing you—the lady or the cat? Never mind, I'll be right there."

With a hoodie shoved over her head to combat the late September chill and her blonde curls crammed into a lopsided bun, Vivian takes off on foot.

To Vivian's absolute dismay, Julian doesn't miss a fucking thing.

When Vivian enters 1005 Custrel Complex through the front door, Julian's eyebrows shoot up. They're high enough to be in danger of joining his hairline soon.

"Have a nice walk?" he asks.

"Sure. It's nice out."

It's not. It's gray, windy, and on the verge of rain. The air is cool enough that Vivian was still shivering in her sweatshirt. Late September in Bristol has autumn in full force.

"Right. Well, do you have any coffee? I could really use another cup before I deal with the corps today." He sighs as though dealing with the corps is the worst punishment Ms. Renee could inflict on him.

"Is that your punishment for breaking your principal? No coffee. I ran out. But we can stop on the way to Ellapond and get some. Where'd you park?" she says quickly.

"In the lot."

This place has a parking lot? Damn, fancy.

"Sounds good, let's go." Vivian tries to herd Julian through the lobby toward the doors. Despite several weeks working together in rehearsals, they don't often touch. Instead, she does her best to use nonverbal body language and facial expressions to indicate that it's time to leave. He doesn't move, and she ends up walking right into him, chest colliding with his side in a way that zings pain through her injured shoulder. She can't help the wince and gasp that escape.

"Why aren't you wearing your sling?"

In her rush to get Julian far, *far* away from anywhere she lives or pretends to live, putting on her sling hardly registered. But she can't exactly say that, so she settles on, "I forgot it."

It's the wrong answer.

"You should be wearing it, Sugar Plum. Let's go get it." His long legs stride across the lobby before Vivian can get an excuse out. He jams the elevator button with a finger before peeking over his shoulder at where she's still gaping at him, desperately trying to plot her way out of this.

But then the elevator dings its arrival, and he enters, politely setting a hand against the metal doors to keep them open for her.

And like an obedient, lying idiot, she follows. The elevator moves as soon as they've entered, presumably responding to the call of another resident—an *actual* resident.

Maybe they can get off on that floor and then she can pretend to have lost her keys on her walk and then . . .

"What floor, Sugar Plum?" Julian's long fingers are hovering over the elevator buttons, poised to select one at her command.

Maybe it's rain in the air, or maybe it's the pain in her injured arm. Maybe it's the way he hasn't told Ms. Renee or anyone else about her lie. Maybe it's temporary insanity. But Vivian's next secret spills out. Unprompted and stark.

"I don't live here."

With shockingly little convincing, Julian coaxes Vivian into taking him to her real apartment. They retrieve her car from the lot, and Julian drives the brief distance to her place. He carefully follows her quiet admissions of, "Turn here," "Make the next left," and, "Park anywhere. There's no lot."

Julian circles the block twice, unable to find a spot that he deems close enough.

Similar to the prior evening, the tension in the car is sharp and unpredictable. The air is charged and heavy, mirroring the impending storm outside. As though either of them could combust at merely an eye roll or harsh word.

Finally, Vivian snaps, "I walked all the way to Custrel from here. I can walk from this block to the building. Just park already."

Neither speaks until Julian has parked, they've exited the car, climbed the stairs to Apt. #4C, she's wiggled her key in the lock *just right*, and she finally throws the door open carelessly. The door swings wide, thumping into the wall next to the fridge when she spits out a tired, "Happy?"

Vivian doesn't watch Julian assess her studio. She doesn't need to see his critical eyes study the low, uneven table that functions as her coffee table, bookcase, dining table, and nightstand. It's mostly neat, but there's scattered ribbons, glue, and sewing supplies from her last pointe shoe surgery session. She doesn't want to know what he thinks of the lumpy green monstrosity that serves as her bed, couch, and chair. She doesn't want to watch him realize that despite her exquisite turns, she's merely another girl, clinging desperately to a childhood dream.

That the day they first met—when she tumbled out of the back seat of her car after the driver's door handle snapped off—wasn't merely an "off" day. Vivian doesn't want to watch Julian pass judgment on her, not again.

"Sit down." He gestures to the pea-green futon, as though he's the host rather than her, before pulling her coffee table away from the couch. He settles himself on the floor, directly in front of her feet.

All at once, tears sting at her eyes, and a fierce tickle itches in her nose. Her throat feels thick and itchy. She's not going to cry. Not after yesterday. *Not again.*

Julian King is sitting on the floor of her studio apartment. All six feet of powerful, lean limbs sitting at her feet in front of her ugly futon. A magnificent zealot kneeling in supplication before an unworthy god. It's unimaginable, and yet, when she skates cautious fingers along his jawline, his stubble is blunt beneath her fingers.

"Please. You don't need to sit there."

"Stop. We need to talk, and I'll feel better if I'm not towering over you."

We need to talk.

He's not her boyfriend. Julian's not even her friend. At best, they're colleagues working toward a common goal. At worst, she's merely a work project to him. A task to complete and check off before moving on.

Principal dancer: trained

The four words shouldn't inspire instantaneous anxiety, yet Vivian can't help the way her heart rate ramps up upon hearing them. The tears from moments ago are now threatening to fall, and he hasn't said anything of substance yet.

"Fine. Let's talk."

Chapter Fifteen

"I know I said we'd only talk about it once, but that was before you let me drop you off at a random building and walked home *injured, in the rain."*

The emphasis he places on the last few words implies that her actions were far graver crimes than simply lying and walking a few blocks. Does he think she murders puppies and babies in her spare time?

"I injured my shoulder, not my leg—"

"Don't start right now," he snaps. Despite his position on the floor, Vivian gets the impression that he is still *very much* in charge of this conversation.

"It seems as though I didn't make myself clear enough yesterday. Circumstances may prevent me from acting upon inclinations I experience, but that doesn't mean that I'll permit—"

In Studio B, Julian can snap his fingers and have everyone in the room dancing at his whims, but here? Now?

"Circumstances may prevent your inclinations and what you'll permit?!" The words spill out of Vivian's mouth in a sharp screech. Is he giving an HR seminar or are they having an honest conversation?

"If you have wisdom to impart, *Mr. Julian*, then spit it out."

And then he's surging up from his spot on her musty carpeted floor to pace the tiny three square feet of unoccupied space. He pulls the hat off his head and angrily spears his fingers into his brown curls, pulling in frustration.

"What do you want me to say, Viv? I'm still coming to terms with the fact that you're not a fucking child! Now you're lying about where you live. What's next? Are you going to tell me you have an alien body double that dances for you? Are you dating Timmer? Is your name even really Vivian?"

Vivian scoffs from her place on the couch.

"And would you put your fucking sling on already? I didn't waste my night in the ER just for you to re-injure it."

That's enough to get her to glue her butt to the futon in spite. "I told you to leave me there! You're the one who wanted to stay! You could've left."

Inexplicably, he deflates.

The tension flies out of him, a bird fleeing out an open window. He melts back to the floor at her feet, and Vivian's stomach twists and twirls. It's been seven weeks since they first met in the parking lot, six weeks since rehearsals began. Compared to her life—or even his—it's a drop in the bucket, a single tear in a flood. And yet, these weeks have been enough that she's begun to learn the curve of his jaw and the meaning behind how often he adjusts his hat.

"That's what you don't understand." Julian leans in to rest his forehead on her knees and the rest of his words are warm against her legs. "I couldn't leave any more than you could quit dancing."

The magnitude of what he isn't saying makes her breath shaky, as though electricity is spiking through her lungs, sparking up her chest and out her parted lips. Somehow, with her conscious decision, her life has come to be made up entirely of leaps and lies.

When Julian settles a warm hand on her knee and tips his head to gaze at her from where it rests in her lap, she does what she always does when he stares at her with his impossible hazel eyes.

She spills her secrets.

"You can get an advance from Ellapond if you need extra for a security deposit on a new apartment."

An advance? Vivian hasn't even gotten her first paycheck. She says as much when he presses, and he mutters darkly under his breath.

"Maureen said the bank needed to validate my account and that it could take a few business weeks."

"You were cast seven weeks ago, and you haven't been paid yet?" Julian asks.

"I tried asking about it during my fitting, but Adelina was there and Maureen assured me that the bank would have it sorted out soon." Saying it aloud, the excuse sounds flimsy, but her fitting with Maureen and Adelina was miserable enough that she wants to recount as little of it as possible.

"Fucking Maureen," he curses under his breath.

"What's that supposed to mean?"

He waves her off, suspiciously refusing to elaborate. "I'll take care of it. You don't have to move once you get paid, but you should know that the option is there."

Despite the mystery his words are shrouded in, his tone and warm palm on her knee are reassuring in the way that few things have been since she first left her parents and moved to Bristol.

It shouldn't come as a surprise, and yet Vivian still startles when two days later her phone dings, notifying her of an updated balance in her checking account. The singular deposit covers payment for all seven weeks since Ms. Renee first cast her back in late August.

Chapter Sixteen

The thing about being dropped from a partner lift is that it comes with a multitude of dilemmas.

Not only does it come with the agonizing itch of being forced to the sidelines while she heals—*Just wait, there's more!*—her injury also comes with an unprecedented anxiety that Vivian's never experienced before. It's not stage fright, normal nerves, or anything mundane. It's a cold, hollow sensation in the pit of her stomach at the thought of Alex's clammy hands lifting her anywhere.

Vivian's shoulder injury forces her to miss a week and a half of rehearsals. After Julian catches her flinching while putting on a jacket one afternoon, he modifies his original declaration of one week. When she's finally allowed back at rehearsal, she learns that she's only permitted to mark the choreography for the next week. Using only a fraction of her energy and skills frustrates her worse than a race-horse forced to be tempered for a young rider. Holding back is miserable.

The final blow lands when she's finally, *finally*, allowed to rehearse as normal, and she finds that she can't. Well, not that she can't dance—never that—but that everything that had been going right in her duet is now broken. Every assisted turn, leap, or lift now has her flinching away from Alex. The memory of his sweaty hands wrenching her shoulder as she fell is a dark specter that haunts every studio space they use.

It comes to head on a Wednesday afternoon. It's Vivian's third day back at full capacity, but the frustration coursing through her body has her nervous as if it's her first day at the barre. Despite usually being her strength, her turns have been sloppy and off-balance all day.

"Okay, enough!" Julian claps his hands as his strong voice rings out from his usual spot near the corner.

Vivian freezes, knees bent and arms prepared to execute another ugly pirouette.

"That will be all, thank you."

Julian's dismissal is precise and final. Vivian's heart sinks into her stomach, an ugly sensation in her chest. She can land clean turns, she *knows* she can. Her whole body deflates when Julian stares at his notebook without further words. Alex is quick to head to the cubbies, gathering his belongings and changing back into his street shoes. But Vivian is rooted in place by the weight of anger and frustration.

"I can step in if you'd like!" Kelsey volunteers from the corner of the room. Julian blinks at her with a vacant expression until she sighs, gathering up her belongings and practically stomping out.

When Julian finally glances up and finds Vivian still standing in the center of Studio C, he blinks at her. Alex and Kelsey have both left, and she's been waiting for several minutes, trying to find the will and courage to spit the words out.

"Your turns are a disaster because you jump out of your skin every time he reaches for you. How is he supposed to assist your turns if he can't touch you, Sugar Plum?"

The words bubble up, the unwanted truth spilling onto the hardwood. "I'm scared."

Julian huffs at her, an airy noise.

"I mean, I know it was an accident. I know he didn't mean to drop me and that even if he lets go while I'm spinning, I'll just land the turn. But I can't help it. It's not a conscious choice. My body remembers his sweaty hands and the pain in my shoulder, and it just reacts. I don't *want* to flinch away," Vivian rambles out, words tumbling across the room before she can bite her lip and force them back down.

"Do you think he can't lift you? That he shouldn't be cast in his role?" Julian's sharp gaze and penetrating questions feel like a trick.

She's careful with her reply. "That's not up to me. I'm the dancer, not the casting director."

"That you are, Sugar." Julian stands, leaving his notebook on his stool.

"I'll work with you—and Timmer—individually. But if I can't get you over the flinching, we'll need to recast. We don't have months to work this out."

"Why?" The surprise of his offer leaves her with little hesitation.

"Because I want to see *you* on that stage, Sugar Plum."

When they meet the following day during what would typically be her duet rehearsal slot, Julian spends *forever* drilling her turns. Over and over she spins, spotting her own eyes in the mirror. Her blonde ponytail slices through the air as she whips her head around to meet her own gaze. She keeps her legs tight, core strong, arms poised but loose.

"Good, but drop your shoulders."

"Meh, you had another in you."

"What the *hell* are you doing with your fingers?"

"One more time."

"One more."

"One more time."

"One last time."

When he finally relents, Vivian's legs are burning with fatigue, her arms are shaky, and she's not sure if she even has toes anymore.

"Okay, now with me."

The words float in and back out of Vivian's awareness as she huffs between tiny sips of water. Too much water, and she'll be spitting it back out in a nauseous fit during the next drill. She learned that the hard way from Ms. Lorraine in high school.

Vivian returns to her spot and awaits further instructions.

Let it be something simple. Please let it be simple.

And then Julian moves toward her until he's standing directly behind her. When he's across the room barking orders or huffing criticisms, it's easy to forget his bulk. Despite lean, graceful limbs, he's tall and strong—easily standing a head above Vivian. As he moves behind her, his silhouette encompasses hers entirely in the mirror. If he were to stand in front of her instead of behind, she'd be invisible.

He left his hat behind on his stool and his brown curls are dented slightly. Vivian wonders if she could remove the dent with her fingers.

"What are you doing?" It's another stupid question. He must bring those out in her.

He quirks an eyebrow when their eyes meet in the mirror.

"How else did you think we were going to practice partnering?"

Clearly, she didn't think through accepting his offer of help *at all*.

When she doesn't reply, Julian continues, "Let's start with assisted pirouettes. Once those are solid, we'll move on."

Vivian nods but it's an automatic gesture, similar to smiling at a waitress or cooing at a puppy. She's sweeping her arms through the air from first when large, warm hands settle on her waist. Every atom of her body stills.

"Let's start with the actual assist. It's what needs the most work, not your turns."

The glance Vivian shoots Julian is sly. "Does that count as a compliment?"

"Did it *feel* like a compliment?"

She doesn't know. She can't feel anything beyond his fingers and palms, so warm they must be searing holes through her leotard.

"Prep?" she asks.

"Start from a passé. Open front and let me turn you."

"You won't drop me?"

"I promise I won't drop you, Sugar."

It takes a dozen tries to get right.

In reality, Vivian could've counted attempt number eight as a win if she hadn't been too distracted by the warm hold of Julian's hands wrapped around her waist, palms and fingers skating over the nylon of her leotard. His grip is a brand, leaving burning skin and wreckage in its wake. Surely, Alex's grip never feels so . . . proprietary?

Attempts nine through eleven go okay but not amazing. Vivian catches a glance of Julian's stupid, dented curls in the mirror at the beginning of attempt nine and she teeters away from his grip instinctively. If anything, the quality of attempts nine through eleven is his fault for being so distracting.

But attempt twelve . . . is something else entirely.

When Vivian finishes it, she sinks into fourth position, and Julian's grip slides up from her waist to wrap around her rib cage, immediately below her breasts.

He squeezes, gently enough she could've imagined it. His touch is electric. She hates the way she craves more of it before he's even released her.

"Good."

This praise *must* count as a compliment.

Chapter Seventeen

Julian's "private coaching"—as Vivian hears it angrily whispered by Kelsey one morning at a company-wide rehearsal—has given him free rein and access to keep her at his beck and call. Vivian has no idea how he's managed to schedule private rehearsals that Kelsey doesn't need to attend, as she's the only swing learning Vivian's choreography, but Vivian doesn't want to invite chaos by asking. Maybe Julian finally overheard one of the rude comments Kelsey makes under her breath every chance she gets. Vivian bites her tongue when he schedules additional one-on-one rehearsals during what used to be her lunch break six days a week.

By the end of their first week of one-on-ones, she's confident that she can perform any assisted or partnered turns without running from Alex or punching him in a blind panic.

In addition to packing her schedule even fuller than she thought possible—or legal—Julian has developed a . . . hands-on approach. Which is the polite way of saying he seems incapable of keeping his hands to himself. It's never obvious enough to be called *inappropriate*, but it's new and that's enough to make Vivian wonder.

Is it a result of her secrets spilling out, or merely a consequence of private rehearsals where they're paired together and he *has* to touch her? Is it a symptom of his admitted interest or an effort to desensitize her to working with a partner? It's only that he keeps doing it when he doesn't absolutely need to, and that feels significant.

As always, he interrupts her thoughts with a hand that brushes over her back as he walks toward the corner to turn on the music.

"I think we've had enough of turns for now, huh?"

Vivian nods even though his back is turned but their gazes catch in the mirror briefly. Their partnered turns are strong. Solid. She's ready to move on.

"Let's try the lift where you fell."

And suddenly she's ready to stick with turns for the foreseeable future. Maybe she can specialize in turns and only turns. Her expression must give away her panic because he's quick to interrupt.

"Nice try with the pout, but it's time. You need to do it and move past it. If you want to dance principal on opening night, you need to figure this out. I've been babying you with the turns, but it's time."

Wait—he's been *babying* her?!

She lets out an indelicate snort before steeling her shoulders. "Fine, let's do it."

When Julian turns to smirk at her, she can see that she's walked right into his trap, a willing victim.

"So, start with the jeté, land, crossover. We prep, I'll lift. Spin down, you land in arabesque, then chaînés away. Got it?" he says in a way that makes it clear the question is rhetorical. He's good at that.

This combination has been haunting Vivian for weeks since her fall. She couldn't forget the steps even if she wanted to. "Yep."

Vivian preps to begin the combination but freezes before her jeté.

"Promise you won't drop me?"

"I won't drop you."

Unlike with her turns, it's not enough of a comfort. She's never had a partner fail her during turns. And even if she had, there's little risk when one foot is still on the floor.

She now knows how it feels to fall from above the head of a grown, gangly man. Knows the heart-wrenching pop of a dislocated shoulder and how the agony of spending weeks on the sidelines is almost worse than the physical pain.

"But do you promise?" The demand is juvenile but it bubbles up all the same.

Julian meets her gaze, eyes clear and resolute.

"I would lie on the hardwood to serve as your landing mat before I ever dropped you."

It rings through the studio as an admission—a vow.

When his stare cuts away and he removes his hat to toss it across the room toward his usual stool, the air crackles with intimacy.

The first three attempts are nonstarters. Vivian twirls away before she even gets within his grasp, refusing to even begin the actual lift.

"I don't know which of us you're trying to tease, but if it's me, it's working," Julian bites out. Vivian rolls her eyes and huffs.

"Again."

"Again."

"Try again."

"I'm going to try again."

"One more."

Then something happens on her ninth try. Vivian leaps and lands. She glides and preps. Julian lifts. Vivian poses. She breathes, he doesn't waver. She rolls, and he dips her. She lands and spins away from him.

And not a single thing goes wrong.

It might not be the most beautifully executed lift in the history of ballet, but she. Fucking. Did. It.

There's a single instance where Vivian and Julian stare across the room at each other, grinning like complete idiots, before she launches herself at him, tears already prickling at her eyes. He catches her with those large hands under her butt when she leaps at him, clinging needier than a baby monkey.

She's smiling while fat, incriminating tears roll down her cheeks. And he's laughing into her neck, warm breath tickling her sweaty skin. She's laughing slightly too because, really, what else is there to do?

After a breath or an hour, Julian pulls back from his new home along her collarbone, and she isn't fast enough to hide the tears. *Where is she supposed to wipe them, his shirt?*

"Come on, Sugar Plum. It wasn't that scary, was it?"

He's still holding her cradled to his chest, and she interlocks her fingers behind his neck and ducks her head into his tee shirt. Julian smells like sweat and spicy cologne. She wants to roll in his shirt until she smells the same.

"No hiding, Sugar. What's wrong?"

Vivian shakes her head, but words don't come easily. "Feelings. And stuff."

She feels his snort more than she hears it, a puff of air tickling her skin, and then they're both moving. His grip on her is solid, and he *did* just lift her whole body above his head so he's probably fine, but she still says, "Sorry. You can put me down. I didn't mean to jump and then cry and . . . "

Her words trail off when Julian settles them both on the floor with her still curled in his lap.

"Apologize for lying about your apartment—or hell, the *other lie*. Don't apologize for being afraid. Not to me."

Tears drip off her chin and onto his shirt when she obediently says, "I'm sorry for lying about my apartment."

But tears quickly turn to huffed laughter when he replies, "Good. Now don't ever act so agreeable again. It's unnatural."

And they sit that way, Vivian's sniffles quieting against his chest with his face tucked into her neck until her muscles and limbs have cooled and stiffened. They're bordering on aching when he finally sighs and pulls back to look at her.

"I'm going to start your rehearsals with Timmer back up."

"Alex? Why?"

Julian's eyebrows jump up. "Why? He's still principal. I've had him rehearsing with Moore, but now that you're getting comfortable, I'd rather swap you in."

Well, that explains the blissful but temporary reprieve from Kelsey . . .

"I know your fear is fresh, but the sooner you work with him, the more time you'll have to iron out hiccups before opening night."

Vivian and Alex haven't spoken since the accident, not *really*. They've danced side by side in company-wide rehearsals since she was cleared by Julian. But since that early rehearsal right after she came back where she flinched away from him the whole time, she's barely seen him. Scarlett told her that he's deeply apologetic, but it's been hard to contend with the envy and discomfort of knowing that even if he made an error, she was the one to suffer. Time and distance have provided space for her to accept what she's always known—the fall was an accident.

She's still not keen to jump into his waiting—clammy—hands after spending a week in Julian's more experienced grip. That's why her heart leaps and soars unnaturally when Julian says, "I've been drilling him constantly with Moore and he's solid. He won't drop you again, I promise."

"You can't promise that. I know it was an accident."

"Viv, in twenty years of dancing, no fall has scared me more. You could've hit your head. You could've torn something. You could've both been injured . . . He will *not* drop you again."

She tries to laugh off the solemnity of his oath. "Twenty years? Are you sure you're going to be able to walk after lifting me like that?"

She's still in his lap. She's sitting in the lap of her . . . instructor? Mentor? Colleague? Whatever the appropriate title is, surely professionalism doesn't extend to include post-rehearsal cuddles.

"Maybe not, but I'm willing to make that sacrifice. Dying beneath you? What a way to go . . . "

Vivian ducks her head, as if that could be enough to hide the blush rising to her cheeks.

"You should start a cooldown though, before you get more than you bargained for." Julian's tone is calm and even, but from where she's sprawled in his lap, a queen atop a muscular throne, she can feel his racing pulse.

"No. I don't think I'm done for the day yet." It's a foolish thought, a foolish comment. But Vivian's always been foolish when it comes to Julian, ever since she tumbled out of her car and began dropping lies like confetti. There's something about his constant challenges that brings out the stubborn streak in her. He makes her want to push back, to earn his praise and her spotlight. It's heart-stoppingly electric.

"No?" Julian arches an eyebrow and adjusts her in his lap, dragging her hips backward to sit closer to his knees and further from his hips. Cool air tickles her torso where it's been dragged away from his. Her leotard clings to her warm skin and the transition from the warmth of his skin to the ambient air leaves her shivering.

The urge to roll and thrust right back to the spot he pulled her away from is blinding. Vivian hates the distance he's placed between them. It's staggering, astonishing, unbearable. The wave of *want* feels insurmountable. Resistance is impossible. Her body is no longer her own, merely an amalgamation of electricity and desire. Beyond the high of a spotlight on stage, it's incomparable.

"No," she gasps out. "I don't want to cool down." *Anything* but that.

"Viv . . ." She can't decide which she prefers rolling off his tongue: Viv or Sugar Plum.

Insane ideas soar through her mind, rockets breaking the sound barrier. She thinks about pushing him down flat on the floor of Studio C. She thinks about pulling on his messy brown curls, licking into his mouth. She wants him to grip her hips hard enough to leave fingerprints.

Wants evidence that this is real, that it's not merely her mind turning daydreams into waking hallucinations. She wants proof—evidence—that the desire burning through her isn't one-sided. That this desperate, foolish want isn't unrequited.

Vivian knows what he said after the ER, after her shoulder, but a declaration of lust isn't the same as intent. If anything, Julian seemed firmly entrenched in the camp of denial and repression. And that was three weeks ago now. Who's to say his feelings haven't changed? Who's to say that his private conversations with Kelsey haven't swayed him in another direction? Who's to say that he isn't sick of Vivian's lies and weaknesses?

But she has to know. The instinct that compelled her to audition for Ellapond—despite the lies it would require and the sacrifices it would demand—rides her heart and body when she reaches a careful, shaky hand to Julian's face.

The expression that stares back at her is devastating, impossibly distraught.

Vivian ghosts her fingertips over the rough stubble of his jawline, over the delicate shell of his ear, and finally up into the disheveled curls that have occupied far more of her mind than she's willing to admit. It's instinct. Simply instinct and adrenaline when she fists her hand in his hair and *pulls*.

"Fuck, Viv. Are you sure? I need you to be sure." Julian's voice is urgent and quick. Almost out of place among their relative stillness. But she understands. She knows with a bone-deep clarity what he's asking. He continues anyway,

"Once I have you, you're mine. That's it for me. So I need you to be certain."

Has she ever been more certain?

There's a squeak, a gasp, and a *thump* in the hallway, and Vivian scrambles backward, crabwalking off Julian's lap as if electrocuted. The reflexive burn of embarrassment stings her cheeks.

When Kelsey sashays through the double doors of Studio C, Julian is standing, relatively composed with his hat back in its rightful place on his head. Vivian is all the way across the room, hurriedly untying her shoes and ripping off her toe pads. Her heart is pounding against her ribs, and it takes too much concentration not to hyperventilate. Kelsey didn't *see* anything. And nothing happened anyway.

"I'll email you next week's schedule," Julian says, ignoring Kelsey.

"Ooh, you're changing the schedule?" Kelsey asks. "That's good because I've been meaning to talk to you . . ."

Vivian nods at Julian without making eye contact and rushes out of the studio as fast as she can, heart thumping erratically. She doesn't bother to stick around long enough to react to Kelsey's hushed whisper of, "Ass-kisser," as she passes.

Part Four

Variation Two

Chapter Eighteen

It's embarrassing in the way that only Vivian can be, apparently.

Do things like this even happen to other people, or does the universe just collect all potentially humiliating events to dispense on her at its will?

There's a second knock on her apartment door, firm and solid. Apparently, her intruder doesn't want to leave her to the peace of icing her aching, blistered feet. It wouldn't be an issue except that she's been exhausted lately. Between extra rehearsals with Alex to drill their lifts and duets, every company rehearsal she's called to attend, and spending her nights desperately trying to fall asleep without thinking about Julian, she's hardly had time to herself. As soon as she slumped on the edge of the stained yellow bathtub in her apartment with her feet in an ice bath, she decided not to move until sleep or hunger forced her. The firm knocks are neither.

And the knocks wouldn't be troublesome except that she's spent so long aimlessly scrolling her phone while seated on the side of the tub, feet slipping into blissful numbness, that it's officially been too long. The welcome reprieve from pain that the ice brought has morphed into the sharp prickles of true numbness. Vivian's facing a hellish blend of pins and needles and hypothermia as she tries to stand from the tub without breaking an ankle.

Wouldn't that be an ironic fate? The fastest principal ballerina career to be ended after a dislocated shoulder and a broken ankle. Surely, the universe doesn't hate her *that* much.

It must hate her at least a little when she exits the bathroom and promptly stumbles down the short hallway to her apartment door. She's wearing a threadbare cardigan thrown over a ratty sports bra and her bleach-stained yoga pants are rolled up to end above her knees. Her feet are unnatural shades of pink and purple better suited to a sunset than human skin. If they weren't feet, they'd make a beautiful sunset. She can just barely feel her legs below the calf. Walking is similar to controlling limbs that don't belong to her—as though she's pulling the strings of a broken marionette, willing it to take even, balanced steps.

Vivian yanks the door open, leaning heavily on the frame to compensate for her inability to stand and wills herself to appear at least infinitesimally more composed than she feels.

From the subsequent snort that Julian releases on the threshold, she fails spectacularly.

"I know you're new as principal, but surely someone has told you that walking is a standard requirement?" he teases. In a heather-blue sweatshirt, a signature black ball cap, and dark gray joggers, he looks far more composed than Vivian. Despite the casual clothes, he's not baring any unnecessary skin nor struggling to stand upright.

Vivian rolls her eyes, unimpressed with his snark. "Are you here to laugh at your own jokes or did you get lost looking for your ego?"

Since he found out—about her age *and* apartment—and since their private rehearsals, everything has been different. They still needle each other at every opportunity, exchanging barbs and sass as though they're on opposing sides of a tennis match. But everything is cut with an edge now. A heightened tension of *what if?*

There's a certain kinship in sharing secrets. The heady, intoxicating rush of being known. It's electric in her veins. Electric in every brush of his hand on her back or click of his tongue in rehearsal. It's novel to share intimacy with a colleague. A superior.

Vivian can't help but wonder if their . . . *moment* last week after rehearsal is simply another secret they'll never speak of. Unless Julian is here to let her down gently? Anxiety bubbles in her stomach at the thought. Only she would get rejected by her older ballet instructor in the precise moment that she's iced her feet for so long that she can barely stand.

"Why are you limping?" He practically barks the words at her, a firm demand for answers.

"It's fine. I just spent a little too long in the ice. What are you doing here?" she replies quickly. If they're going to have an uncomfortable conversation, she'd prefer to get it over with. Rip the bandage off and all that.

"Come on." And then he's herding her through the door and over to her ugly futon.

She's barely settled onto it when he's grabbing one of her bright pink feet in his warm hands and kneading. "Shit! Your feet are freezing. How long did you ice them for?"

He kneels at her feet again, startlingly similar to that day merely a week ago, when he returned her car after the accident. Seeing a man of his size and demeanor kneeling at her feet—her red frozen toes and splotchy purple ankles—is drastically unsettling. It's counterintuitive to everything she thought she knew about him. And yet he keeps doing this. He pushes and pushes but when it comes down to it, he's kneeling at her frozen feet. If it was a movie scene, she'd call it poetic.

"It's fine. They'll warm up. Why are you here?"

"I wanted to talk about Friday."

Friday, when she managed to recreate the lift that's been haunting her since her injury. Friday, when she cried into his chest in relief and elation. Friday, when he cradled her in his lap, and she gripped his hair with violence and need.

Friday.

Her confidence and bluster disappear with that single word. "Ahh, okay. If it's about rehearsals with Alex, you could have emailed me. You didn't have to deliver the schedule in person. Not on a weekend."

His fingers skate over the arch of her left foot, and it sends sharp needles up her calf, nerves sparking with electricity and the growing awareness of sensation.

"You know it's not about the schedule," he replies.

Julian sighs, hands stilling on her feet. She can't believe he's touching her again. Can't believe his fingers aren't numb yet from the chill of her skin.

"It was one thing when I thought you were too young. I mean, you're still too young—"

Vivian is quick to interrupt, as if the speed of her argument will be enough to sway him. As if saying you aren't *that* young does anything but sound self-proving.

"Twenty-four is not the same as fifteen."

Julian nods, brown curls bouncing. "It's not. But I'm thirty-five, Sugar Plum."

She'd guessed his age after their trip to the ER, but she hadn't known it exactly until now. Vivian can't help but remember that Kelsey is only seventeen.

"Fifteen is not twenty-four, but neither is thirty-five. And number games aside, I'm still your instructor."

"You're technically an artist-in-residence. Ms. Renee handles casting."

"With my input."

Vivian huffs, tired of this game. "What do you want me to say? Okay, you're my instructor. You're old. Congratulations, Old Man! You win." She wiggles the fingers of both hands at him in a mockery of celebration.

A sharp flick to her slowly warming foot leaves her wincing.

"Watch it, Sugar. I'm not trying to fight with you."

"Then what are you trying to do?" Vivian tries to stand on her wobbly feet, tries to escape his kneading grip and his sharp hazel eyes, but he's quick to wrap strong hands around her ankles.

"I'm trying to make sure you understand what you're getting yourself into."

Everything is electric, bubbles and little shocks that thicken the air of her studio. Breathing through the haze, she asks, "And what am I getting myself into?"

Chapter Nineteen

She knows. She *knows*, but to believe it—to trust in the improbability—seems impossible. It seems dangerous. Will certainty be enough to save her from the broken heart that surely lingers on the horizon?

But Julian reads her, reads her probing question and insecurity as though he already knows the end of the story before opening the book.

She thinks he'll speak, thinks he'll drop another of his earth-shattering confessions on her, but when he leans into her chilled legs from his spot on the ground, it's entirely unexpected. Julian licks her shin.

He licks a broad stripe up her shin and sets his teeth against her kneecap delicately before she manages to choke out any words.

The air of her apartment is thicker than soup, and Julian—*Mr.* Julian—is kneeling on the ugly carpeted floor of her dingy studio, licking and nibbling her legs. Vivian wants to scream. She wants to throw him out or throw herself at him.

"When you said I didn't know what I was getting myself into, I didn't realize that you were looking for a chew toy."

"I've always admired your sharp tongue. Even when your nerves are written across your face for anyone to see, you always have something smart to say."

"I imagine hearing something smart is quite novel for you."

"Bold words for a woman about to hyperventilate," Julian retorts.

And when he bites at her thigh with a touch more pressure, Vivian is close to gasping for air. Despite countless hours of rehearsals, she's never been so winded.

He's only touched her icy feet, only licked and bitten at her calves, and yet the electricity is unbearable, the tension undeniable. He's barely even ventured above her knees. If he touches her—*really* touches her—she might scream. She'll give him anything he asks for.

"You have a lot of arrogance for a man on his knees."

"Does it truly seem as though *I'm* the vulnerable one?" asks the arrogant asshole.

"Is this a lecture or a fuck?"

Vivian wants to smack herself the moment the words slip out. Despite her brave face and sass, she knows she's in over her head. Vivian hasn't had many partners, not when dance quickly became a priority for her in middle school, but she's had enough to know that there's plen-ty she *doesn't* know. But it's not Julian's age or pre-sumed experience that overwhelms her, it's something fundamentally intrinsic to *him*. He walks into a studio, and her heart beats a little faster. He praises her grand jeté, and her breath catches. The mere idea of sex with him is so beyond plausible that it's all she's thought about. There's safety in improbabilities. In chasing un-likely dreams and striving for unattainable goals.

Julian shoots her a slanted grin that screams of sin and debauchery.

"Fine, take your pants off."

He doesn't move from his spot in front of the futon, leaving her to awkwardly lift her hips and wriggle her yoga pants down until they're pooling around her an-kles. She moves quickly, lest logic rears its dangerous head.

The instant her loose sweats and underwear pool around her ankles, Julian stares with hungry eyes.

"Last chance to back out," he offers without pausing his study of her newly bared skin.

"Or what? You'll stare me to death?" Vivian doesn't back down. She couldn't peel his fingers from her legs if she wanted to, couldn't remove his touch any more than she could remove her own limbs.

Julian doesn't reply. He nips her right above her knee before dragging her hips to the edge of the futon with strong fingers. He leans in, stubble pressing right against her core for one impossibly long breath.

Then there's a *sharp* bite to her clit that leaves her whimpering and electric. It's more of a retort than anything he could have vocalized. She's immediately wet.

Vivian's hands drop to Julian's head, and she's quick to knock his hat aside and delve her fingers into his brown waves. That seems to be all the approval he needs because he settles in at her feet, ostensibly intent on devouring her whole—one tantalizing lick at a time.

Unlike some of Vivian's past experiences, Julian is fervent between her legs. As though licking and sucking at her rewards him more than her. His enthusiasm is heady, swelling Vivian's body with confidence and surety. To know that this difficult, caring, cranky, impossible man wants her is one thing. To experience the full force of his desire is something else entirely. To see Julian on his knees as a devout worshipper is intoxicating. Addictive. Vivian knows she'll remember the sight for the rest of her life.

The stubble on his chin and cheeks prickles at her. He licks, nibbles, sucks, and laves, testing out spots and techniques while studying her reactions with keen eyes. As much as she will forever remember Julian kneeling for her, she knows he's memorizing her in turn.

She watches for as long as she can until the dizzying spirals of pleasure from his mouth force her eyes to close. Vivian thinks she might be shaking. Maybe it's the futon shaking, maybe it's Julian.

When he seals his mouth over her clit and *sucks*, she can't help but let out an airy, *"Fuck, Julian."*

He rumbles in response, and the vibration feels delicious.

"More, please. *More.*"

Her hips twitch and flex under his hold, little thrusts of desperation. It's so, *so* good, but it's not quite enough.

When Julian pulls his mouth back to gaze up at her, his stubbled chin is shiny and wet. She hopes the friction burns from his facial hair last forever.

"What do you need?"

Embarrassment heats her cheeks at the question, but it's not enough to stop her pleading response of, "Your fingers. Please."

"If I'd known that a few licks would make you so polite, I would've dropped to my knees in Studio C weeks ago."

Vivian snorts indelicately, and a corresponding chuckle rumbles out of Julian. Vivian's never had sex like this. Never had a partner who made her burn up inside one moment and laugh carelessly the next. That he should be off-limits only seems fitting.

Her soaring amusement melts back into rapture at the first touch of his fingers. Julian delivers a sharp tap to her clit before sliding two fingers into her. The sensation is bliss. Vivian's whole world is wet, warm, and charged. A decadent bubble bath. The joy of screaming at the top of a mountain.

Her hips rock of their own accord now, chasing her peak. Julian moans against her wet skin, laving her clit with broad strokes of his tongue as his fingers pump.

He curls his fingers, applying pressure just where she needs it most, as he sucks her clit into his mouth, rolling it gently between his teeth.

Vivian explodes and the world is champagne bubbles that send jolts of ecstasy everywhere.

"Don't stop. Don't stop. Don't stop," she begs, fingers tightening in his hair. She couldn't release him if she tried. Simply couldn't allow him to exist anywhere but between her thighs.

For all that Julian's pushed and challenged her in the weeks they've known each other, he's uncharacteristically cooperative now. He doesn't stop, curling his fingers tighter, sucking her more sharply.

And then Vivian crests, flooding into his mouth.

By the time her limbs stop trembling and she has the wherewithal to blink down at Julian, he's wiping her wetness off his chin and licking it off his palm.

"You should've warned me you're a squirter," he says with a quirked eyebrow.

She lacks the coordination to shrug and instead huffs out a breath that could mean anything.

He continues anyway, "I don't mind. God no, that was the hottest fucking thing I've ever seen. But if I'd known, I'd have put a towel down first."

Now that she thinks about it, the lumpy futon does feel awfully damp beneath her.

"I didn't..."

In spite of everything, Vivian has a heart-stopping moment of hesitation.

"It's never happened before?" Julian guesses.

"No, that's not it. But it's only happened once before. With my ex . . . girlfriend."

Vivian waits for a reaction. Waits for Julian to bring up the way he's likely seen her staring at Ms. Renee in some inexplicable combination of awe and attraction during rehearsal. Waits for something that sounds polite but carries disdain.

Instead, he bites right above her knee, sucking on the skin until there's a bright, flushed stain.

"Let's get you cleaned up."

Julian stands and walks to the bathroom and Vivian's certain her heart goes with him.

He's gone for what could be a second or an hour when she hears the bathroom pipes give a telltale squeak that means the shower is running. He appears back in front of her before she can be surprised that he's helping himself to a shower.

"As much as I'd love to climb in with you, your shower is barely large enough for one adult. Trying for two seems dangerous. Wait another minute before you get in though, there was still some ice in the tub that needs to melt."

Oh.

Oh.

The shower is for her.

"You don't want to . . . clean up first?" she asks. He and the futon suffered the brunt of the . . . mess after her orgasm.

"No. You go first. I'll try to dry the futon. Does the cover come off?"

When Vivian stands, there's an incriminating wet spot at the edge of the ugly green fabric. At least it's not in the center where she typically sleeps.

"Uhh, I don't think so. Are you sure you don't want to . . . uhh, wash your face before I shower?" she asks again.

Julian grins at her, bright and broad, and she thinks she might be seeing stars. Maybe she's having a heart attack? Surely, the erratic beat of her pulse can't be healthy. His grin is dazzling. She'll do anything to see it again.

"Viv, if I thought you wouldn't get mad, I'd never wash my face again. I'd grow a beard so that every time I ate you, I'd get to smell you for hours after."

And that's . . . a lot. She can't remember being speechless before, but there's something about Julian's ardent passion that leaves her in awe. Her dreams of a dance career mean that she understands the concept of mindlessly pursuing of a goal. But to be the goal . . . to be the subject of all that focus and infatuation is more than she could've imagined.

"You're welcome between my legs any day, but please, still wash your face."

Julian chuckles and ushers her into the bathroom where the peeling wallpaper has collected condensation and steam, thanks to the broken ceiling fan.

Chapter Twenty

Vivian should've known better than to leave Julian unsupervised in her apartment. It's not that he hasn't been in it before. And it's not that she's left anything too embarrassing for him to find. The issue is that there isn't all too much for him to find.

When he'd visited before, he'd clearly thought her place was small and rundown. Fortunately, she'd failed to give him a tour, and he didn't realize to what extent her studio is . . . lacking.

Vivian finds him scowling down at the ugly green futon with a dish towel in hand when she exits the bathroom.

"I know it's not pretty, but what did my futon ever do to you?"

But when Julian finally drags his hazel gaze up to meet hers, there's something admonishing and indescribable boring into her. "Where's your bedroom, Sugar Plum?"

Vivian drops her eyes, fidgeting with the drawstring on her clean sweatpants. "You're looking at the bedroom. And the kitchen, living room, dining room, and foyer. Not the closet though, that's over there," she says, gesturing at the door that he must have previously assumed led to the bedroom. "Never seen a studio before?"

His hat's back in its rightful place, a touch crooked and backward atop his mussed hair. Vivian wants to pull it back off and see how much messier she can make his curls.

He claps his hands, and it's a little too reminiscent of their countless shared rehearsals. "Pack a bag. We're not spending the night on your wet couch."

"I know you've probably never seen a futon in real life before, but there's no reason to insult it. It's a true innovation of furniture if you think about it. Something that can serve as a couch or a bed or a chair. Sometimes a table too, if you're careful."

Julian stares at the pea-green futon with disgust. "I'd rather burn that thing than sleep on it."

"Well then, it's awfully presumptive of you to assume I'd share it with you. Who invited you to spend the night anyway?" Vivian throws the words at him defensively, insecure about his obvious disdain for her sleeping arrangements.

She's not particularly enthusiastic about her studio apartment either, but she signed her lease before getting cast by Ellapond, and it's only been a few weeks since regular paychecks have started rolling in after the "bank issue." Between rehabbing her shoulder, extra rehearsals with Julian to work on lifts and partnering, and her normal *extra full* schedule of rehearsals, she's lacked the time and effort to worry about upgrading her furniture, much less researching other apartments. It's a sore spot.

"Quit glaring at me and pack a bag already," Julian says, waiting impatiently.

"Uhh, where exactly do you think I'm going? And I'm tired anyway. Can we argue about this some other time?"

"Yeah, Viv, we can argue later. At my place. In an actual bed."

She's stuffing a change of clothes and some toiletries into a well-loved backpack, even as she rolls her eyes at him. Sleeping alone is overrated. "A real bed? And where will you be sleeping then?"

"Hopefully, right under you if I have my way."

If he'd led with the promise of more sex, she would've gotten on board much faster. When she tells him as much, he only lets out another of those heartbreaking laughs that make her wonder if she can squeeze in round two before they leave.

Chapter Twenty-One

For all of Julian's apparent contempt for her cramped studio apartment, the car ride to his place is shorter than expected. They ride together in his car after he tells her in no uncertain terms that her car is "one more inch of rust away from disintegration." After an orgasm and shower, Vivian finds that she's notably less motivated to fight him on it.

He drops a hand onto her thigh as he drives, settling long fingers over the curve of her quad. Julian lives closer to Ellapond than her, on a domestic-looking street boasting quaint townhouses with matching front yards. The driveway he pulls into has a maroon mailbox and a tree that occupies most of the small front yard. Thanks to the recent October weather, the foliage is vibrant, and leaves have only just begun to collect along the sidewalk. Thanks to the picturesque townhomes and the golden lampposts glowing in the early evening light, the street looks akin to an autumn catalog rather than a real neighborhood that her duet instructor calls home.

Julian hustles her out of the car, ushering her through the garage and into the house. As soon as he's locked the door behind her and hung his car keys on a nearby hook, he's pressing her back against the door. He pins her between the warmth of his body and the unyielding door.

And then he kisses her, open-mouthed and fierce, as though earlier was merely an appetizer. It strikes her then that despite the way he fell to his knees for her earlier, despite their *moment* in Studio C on Friday, they haven't kissed until now. Improbable yet true, just like them.

Julian tastes sharp, like mint, as she kisses him back, fisting a hand in his jacket and pulling. Even pressed against her, he's not close enough. She wants more. Always more.

It isn't until he chuckles against her lips that she realizes she's been quietly voicing her desires aloud with a desperate, needy chant of, "More, more, more."

"And here I thought my mouth made you polite?" Julian teases.

"Fine. More, *please*," Vivian answers, nipping at his bottom lip.

"Oh, that's much better," he purrs. "Now tell me what you want."

Instead of replying, Vivian mouths at his neck and slips a hand down the front of his joggers, teasing the skin of his lower stomach with the very tips of her fingers.

"You." The second it's out of her mouth, it feels cliched and trite. Surely, that line won't work on a man like him.

Yet when he surges in to close the distance between them, licking right into her mouth in a manner that suggests far more lewd and delicious things, she's proven wrong. It's galvanizing.

Julian kisses fiercely, as if he intends to consume her entire being, beginning with her mouth. She kisses him back, tangling her fingers in his hair and pulling, pulling, *pulling*, until he lets out a groan that sounds as desperate as her own racing heartbeat.

"Up," he orders with a swat at her thigh. His hands are quick to catch her under her thighs when she jumps and clings to him. He's blindly carrying her up the stairs, nibbling at her neck all the while before she can process how many floors the townhouse spans.

After a brief stop on a landing for wet nips to her neck and even more stairs, Vivian is gently dropped on a fluffy duvet covering a bed that immediately puts her ugly futon to shame. The cotton is smooth and crisp under her back and if a hungry-looking Julian wasn't staring down at her, she'd be tempted to settle in for a nap.

"Pants off," Julian orders without looking up from where he's already undressing himself.

"Only my pants?" Vivian sasses. Years of tireless rehearsals and workouts have left her body petite and slim.

Her breasts are nothing extraordinary, but keeping her baggy hoodie on doesn't sound sexier than removing it.

"Everything," Julian quickly corrects. "Take off everything, but pants first."

The instructions immediately make sense when he drops to kneel next to the bed, tugging her to the edge, and splays her thighs over his shoulders.

He dives in to lick her indulgently, and she's struck again that this—the seemingly selfless act of dropping to his knees for her—might be for his pleasure just as much as hers.

Propping herself up on her elbows, Vivian sits up to stare down at Julian where he's delivering his tithe, one lick at a time. His chest is bare and broad, his warm olive complexion is smattered with a hint of bronze hair over his pectorals and sternum. Muscles flex and straighten as he lifts a hand to spread her lips, spearing her with his tongue.

She's electric, as though a high-voltage current is running directly from his mouth into her body. Vivian can hardly bear it. She never wants it to end.

She wants more and yet cannot imagine what she'll do if she gets it. Can she stand more?

It's not until Julian pulls back and mumbles soft re-assurances into the thin skin of her hip crease that she realizes she's whimpering, a soft, high-pitched sound that she'd denounce as pathetic if she had the where-withal to speak.

"More, please," she begs, incapable of surviving without Julian's mouth on her flesh.

"Yeah, baby, you can have more, but you have to relax. Lie back for me," Julian soothes.

Vivian is quick to drop down from her elbows, the bed a soft comfort at her back. She can't reach Julian's hair, so she fists her hands in the duvet, gripping and clenching instinctually.

"Do you wanna come?" Julian taunts with the most delicate, soft, unsatisfying lick to her clit. Vivian wants heat. She wants pressure and sensation and electricity. She wants to absorb Julian into her skin until they are sharing the current coursing through her. She wants *more*.

"More. *Please*," she groans out. "You're being cruel."

He huffs against her, air tickling her sensitive skin in the meanest way.

"Me? Cruel? What happened to the prim and polite Vivian who says please and thank you so nicely?" the asshole taunts.

Vivian groans, now frustrated. "She's waiting for you to do something worthy of praise."

Since they first met, Vivian's always known that her sass and back talk would get her in trouble with Julian one day. It was inevitable. But she never expected that it would be *today*.

Karma comes with a swift, sharp smack to her clit.

In retrospect, he must have pulled back his strength because the smack hardly hurts.

The novelty and shock of the action, though? That has her moaning and arching up toward him, desperate for another touch, whether it be gentle or harsh.

"Fuck. Did you like that? You drive me insane, Sugar. When you challenge and push me, I go insane trying not to push back until you're at the edge. But then as soon as I get my hands on you, you're as polite and submissive as can be. Which is it? Are you acting out for attention?" he asks.

Is she?

It's never been intentional. She doesn't mean to challenge him, to poke, prod, and banter. It's hardly a choice. He simply inspires it in her. Something about him begs her instincts to push back, to respond with bold ferocity. She feels more herself than ever.

When she tells him as much, he laughs into her skin and the rumble is an earthquake to her heart.

"Well, you have my attention now."

And when he returns his face to her, sucking on her clit as he slips two fingers into her, she can tell that she does.

His fingers curl and caress inside her until she's shaking and sweating, too blissed out to do anything but writhe.

"Come all over my face, baby. Get me nice and wet."

His fingers pump and press as he nibbles her clit slightly too hard, and it's *perfect*. She's exploding, cresting, and soaring. A never-ending fireworks display.

When Julian finally drags his face from her skin, his mouth and chin are shiny and wet in a manner that's becoming dangerously familiar and addictive.

Chapter Twenty-Two

"I could get used to you kneeling for me," Vivian says when she finally catches her breath.

Julian's rearranged her securely on his bed, legs no longer dangling off the edge. He's looming over her though, all lithe, warm skin, and tented boxer briefs. His dark hair is messy, curls askew and doing their best to defy gravity and reason. His chin and the dark stubble that calls it home are shiny with moisture. Combined with his disastrous curls and uneven smirk, the effect should be silly. Instead, it's breathtaking.

She still wants more. He's made her insatiable.

"So much for no more smart-ass comments," he says, voice raspy and low.

"You'll have to do better than a few licks if you want to shut me up," she retorts.

Why can't she keep her mouth shut around this man? More than only pushing her within the walls of Ellapond, he pushes her within herself. Rubbing her in all the wrong—and right—ways until she's stretching. Forcing her to grow into herself. Inspiring her to spotlight the boldest version of Vivian, the one that's spent twenty-four years waiting in the wings. The version desperate to take center stage. In every sense of the meaning.

Sex with Julian feels like a whole lot more than just sex.

"'Better than a few licks.'" He scoffs. "That's what we're calling it now? If you want better than a few licks, you'll have to tell me what you have in mind. I only hope I can live up to the lofty expectations of the Sugar Plum Fairy."

For all the versions of Julian that she's seen so far—cranky morning rehearsal Julian, evil demon Julian who makes her do extra shoulder rehab, pushy and concerned Julian from the hospital and after—almost-naked teasing Julian might be her absolute favorite.

When he slips out of his boxer briefs and tosses a foil packet onto the bed next to her, Vivian immediately reevaluates. Naked Julian is her favorite Julian.

"You should always be naked," Vivian says, completely ignoring his earlier taunts about her *expectations*.

"Always?" he asks, the corner of his mouth creeping upward as he leans in to steal a kiss.

As Vivian admires all the warm skin on display, she fights the urge to nod robotically. His career has gifted Julian with defined strength, while age has given him a rugged softness. Enough imperfections to appear human.

Except for his cock. It hangs long and heavy, reddish head curling slightly left. His cock looks perfect.

"Definitely. Clothes on you is a crime."

"I'll keep that in mind."

He's nodding along with the nonsense she keeps spewing by default. She rambles about how she supposes he can wear socks in winter, but maybe if he always stays indoors with her, there would be no need for clothes. All the while, he nibbles down her neck before getting distracted by a freckle near her left nipple.

"Are you still wet for me, sweetheart?"

Vivian's fairly certainly that she's wetter than she's ever been. It'll be a miracle if she isn't soaking his sheets.

"That depends. If I say yes, what are you going to do about it?"

Julian groans into her chest, the rumbling air tickling her sensitive skin.

"Sugar, I don't think I can wait much longer."

Wait for what? Vivian doesn't know what they're waiting for, but if he doesn't want to wait, then neither does she.

Julian pulls back from her breast, hazel eyes shining down at her before his gaze drops to her lap where he's watching . . .

Vivian jolts at the sudden warm flesh swiping at her clit and she sits up to follow his gaze down, down, down. He's tapping the head of his cock against her clit. A staccato beat of liquid heat.

There's something about it. Something about the way their skin slides and catches and the way he can't seem to pull his eyes away from the sight. Vivian's letting out a soft moan before she can help herself.

"In me, in me, in me. Please, Julian."

With those soft taps and his molten gaze, he's reduced her to a begging mess. Again.

"Fuck, okay. Hang on, Sugar Plum."

And then he pulls away, tearing open the foil packet and sliding a condom on at a speed that almost looks painful.

Vivian waffles briefly, wondering if she should remain upright or lie back down. Right when she's decided to lie down but hasn't figured out how to do so gracefully without flopping awkwardly, Julian kisses her. The distraction is immediate and all-encompassing.

Julian notches himself, and when he slides in, they both sigh.

Between the pressure, the heat, the sensations, and *Julian*, Vivian finds herself wholly overwhelmed. Then he thrusts, a rhythmic, rolling motion that rocks their bodies together. Vivian moans into his mouth, a desperate noise that he sucks down wholeheartedly. She's so wet that there's no resistance as he continues to thrust into her, their skin sliding together and apart when she bucks up to meet his hips. Julian and his stupidly perfect cock fill her perfectly. He's slightly larger than her last partner, but the stretch feels exquisite. As though stretching her is merely another way of pushing her to be *more*.

It's good. It's really fucking good. Apparently, that's still not enough for Julian-fucking-King and his impossible standards.

"What do you need, Sugar? Tell me what you need," he croons, face buried in her hair.

She hums a nonsensical acknowledgment but fails to form words.

"Viv, fuck. I can't last with you. And I want you to come for me one more time."

After two orgasms and the electrifying experience of being his sole focus, there's nothing that she truly *needs*, but if he's asking, there are plenty of things that she wants.

"Rub my clit. Please," she gasps, breathless and desperate.

Vivian isn't new to sex. She isn't a blushing virgin or an inexperienced child. Between her on-and-off high school boyfriend, Marcus, her relationship with Kyla when she first moved to the city, and a handful of one-night stands, she's had sex before. Some of it was even good sex. Some of it was even *really good*.

It all still pales in comparison to the obsessive tenacity that Julian levels her way. As an instructor, he's always been critical and intense. Always pushing her limits and boundaries, molding her to be stronger, sharper, braver.

Here and now, rocking his hips into hers as he flicks her clit just shy of too hard, that intensity hasn't waned in the slightest. It's heady and consuming, and Vivian has undoubtedly never had sex like *this*. He assesses her with careful, studying eyes that she knows are cataloging her every preference. He touches her with rough possession, grip sure and certain.

Three more sharp flicks to her clit and Vivian comes again, twitching and moaning under Julian.

With a handful more of those rolling undulations, Julian's chanting into her neck, breath hot and damp.

"Viv. Viv. Fuck, Sugar."

When the shudders and twitches have subsided, he pulls out, disposing of the condom with a sleight of hand that would be comical if she wasn't out of breath. He's herded her into the bathroom for a quick cleanup and then back into his bed—properly in it this time—before she has time to protest at the indignity. He arranges her on the bed, curled on her side in a mountain of pillows before spooning her tightly.

She laughs at his assumed impropriety. "Guess I'm definitely staying the night then?"

"I didn't have you pack that bag for nothing."

"I have a meeting with—" He's quick to wrap a warm palm over her mouth, silencing her protest.

"I know. I'll drive you in the morning. Now go to sleep before I change my mind and keep you up all night."

Liquid heat runs through Vivian's stomach, stronger than a shot of liquor on an empty stomach. He's intoxicating.

She squirms slightly against him, acutely aware of how *empty* she feels without him.

Julian sighs into her hair, blonde wisps tickling her neck from his breath. "What is it, Sugar Plum?"

She squirms again, their warm, naked bodies pressed too tightly for her to ignore the heat.

"I think I should put some clothes on." But she doesn't move—doesn't pull from his embrace or make any effort to locate her overnight bag.

"Do you really want to get dressed?"

She doesn't. She doesn't want to get dressed. Doesn't want to add layers of fabric or distance between them. But she feels crazy. Feels like she's onstage in front of thousands. Feels like she's riding the high of applause and adrenaline. Feels like she's terrified that she'll never ride this high again. She tries to hold still, barely daring to inhale for fear of wiggling around again and annoying him.

When she doesn't reply, the hand on her hip tightens. "What is it, Viv?"

Awkwardly, stupidly, she blurts out the first thing that comes to mind.

"I'm so empty."

It might be the worst truth she's ever admitted to him. The most vulnerable and bare she's allowed herself to be.

But just the same as every other secret she's spilled to him, Julian reacts in the impossible—perfect—way that only he can.

The hand on her hip slides over to her belly and then down until he's sliding two warm fingers into her.

"Is that it, Sugar? You need something in your wet little pussy to go to sleep?"

She doesn't. She's never tried to sleep with something or some*one* inside of her.

"No. I—"

Julian shushes her, somehow both sweet and condescending. "Sleep, Viv."

And somehow, with two of Julian's fingers curled inside her, she does.

Part Five

The Coda

Chapter Twenty-Three

Vivian wakes up horny.

But it isn't simply that she wakes up horny. She wakes up with Julian's fingers parting her lips before sliding over her slit. With the way he's pressed up behind her, hard cock nestled and rocking between her ass cheeks, it's no surprise that she's wet. His fingers dip into her, gathering her moisture before pulling back out. She never managed to get dressed before falling asleep, and she's never been more thankful for her nudity.

"Open up, Sugar," Julian says, wet fingers tapping at her bottom lip.

Vivian opens her mouth on instinct, body loose and pliant with sleep.

"What time is it?" she mumbles around the fingers in her mouth. They're thick and warm. His skin tastes of salt and something distinctly feminine—her flavor.

"You have somewhere to be?" Julian teases, fingers pumping in and out of her mouth. An imitation she'd rather he follow through with somewhere other than her mouth.

"Meeting with Ms. Renee at 9:30," she chokes out.

Julian sighs into her hair and pulls his hand away, snaking it down her neck to pluck at a taut nipple.

"I know. I didn't forget. But if you can still remember, I'm not working hard enough."

"How long have you been working at it now?" Vivian asks, wondering what she may have missed since falling asleep with his fingers curled inside of her and waking up to find them sneaking back in.

How long did he play with her before she woke up? What did he do while she was asleep, warm and compliant?

Her stomach twists at the intersection of unfamiliarity and blazing arousal in a new and truly terrifying way. The thought of him touching her while she slept is more than she'd ever known to ask for but everything she could want. Instead of arrogant and irritating, his presumed comfort with her body is electrifying. As if he heard her complaint of emptiness the night before and managed to hear everything she wasn't saying.

"Don't worry, Viv. I saved all the excitement until you woke up."

Vivian snorts and rolls further onto her stomach, trapping Julian's hand where it's dipped into her bellybutton.

"Are you gonna keep teasing me? I'm falling back asleep," she mumbles, not tired in the least.

"You just go back to sleep then, sweetheart," Julian teases. He wiggles his hand out from underneath her and uses it to hike her knee up, thighs slipping past each other to bare her to the cool room.

His weight shifts on the bed, there's a telltale crinkle, and then he's notching that perfect cock at her slit. Two swipes spread her wetness around until they're both saturated, and then he's sliding in without resistance.

Face down on his bed, the angle is vastly different from the night before. Julian's thrusts are shallow, but they zing something inside her that sends fireworks through her veins. She thought last night was a miracle, but now she knows it was only the beginning.

Vivian moans, light and airy as his hips snap downward, pelvis meeting the cushion of her ass. Sex like this feels lewd. Carnal. Impossibly decadent.

"Oh, you like it like this, Sugar Plum? You like it when I press your face into the pillow and pound your pussy?"

But Vivian's the one who rolled over onto her stomach, and he has definitely *not* been trying to suffocate her. Despite his words, she put herself in this position of submission. When she lifts her head to tell him as much, he lands a sharp swat on her ass cheek before she can get out more than a muffled, "You didn't—"

"Unless you're saying 'thank you' or 'more,' I think I've had enough of your sass for now," Julian says. With a delicious rhythm, the head of his cock making tight circles inside her, it's improbable that he should manage such eloquence.

"Shut *up*," Vivian chokes into the pillow.

"You're shaking, Viv. That feel good?" he asks, ignoring her words. His deep voice is warm and smug, blatantly teasing.

She shakes. Just a slight tremble across her body, as if her veins are full of Pop Rocks instead of blood.

"Mmhguhhfk," she chokes out.

With his size advantage, he could press her into the mattress. He could suffocate her and take what he wants. He could crush her, but instead, he's rambling, crooning dirty words in a husky voice.

Julian chuckles against the back of her neck, large palms braced on either side of her head.

"Whatever you say, Viv," Julian answers patronizingly.

"Mmhg. Fuuck."

"Just a little more for me, sweetheart. You can last a little longer, can't you?"

She can't. She's pretty sure she's already coming. It's different from her orgasms the night before. Different from the way she trembled and gasped under his tongue. But her bones are melting to liquid, and she's lost control of her limbs. Lost control of her words.

Everything is hot, liquid bliss. The world all obscure heat and pleasure.

Vivian wakes up in Julian's arms again.

She blinks through heavy, crusted eyelids to the sound of her name whispered softly from above.

"Come on, Viv. You'll kill me if you miss your meeting."

"Huh?"

"You have a 9:30 with Renee, remember?"

That's enough to have her sitting up, the fluffy duvet falling to her lap. She flinches, prepared to pull it back up to cover herself, only to find that she's drowning in a deep maroon crewneck she's admired on Julian before. She does *not* remember getting dressed.

Vivian's quick to spring out of his bed, grabbing her overnight bag before hiding in the bathroom. By the time she's dressed, freshened up, and ready to leave for her meeting, Julian is waiting with a travel mug full of warm coffee in the kitchen. He grabs his car keys from the hook near the garage and ushers her out without a word.

It's not until they're idling at the stop sign right beyond his neighborhood that he finally speaks.

"Guessing things got a little intense for you last night?" Julian asks. From his relaxed grip on the steering wheel, he doesn't appear too worried about her response.

"Uhh, yeah. I—Well, when we were . . . " she trails off, not sure how to admit that she thinks she *fell asleep* during sex. Maybe it was technically after her orgasm but yeah. Who does that? Sure, she's been killing herself at rehearsals lately, but still . . .

"It's okay. Drink your coffee."

She eyes him, his deep green fleece and brown ball cap making him appear the ideal lumberjack to fit in the picture-perfect catalog of his townhouse's neighborhood. Vivian takes a deliberately audible gulp of the coffee he made her. It's hot and just sweet enough. Once she's made a show of loudly sipping at the perfect beverage, Julian finally says, "Was it okay for you?"

Vivian snorts. Honest to god snorts, practically choking on the coffee. She'd expected more arrogance and swagger from him rather than this calm concern.

"Yeah, it was 'okay' for me," she answers, teasing him with gentle air quotes. "I think you may have melted my brain though. I didn't mean to fall asleep right after."

"It wasn't too much?" This time, the question comes quickly, as though he's too eager for an answer to let her finish speaking.

"Uhh—" Vivian clears her throat, staring down at her lap with a prickle of tension. "I feel bad that I fell asleep, and you had to dress me, but aside from that . . . *itwasthehottestsexofmylife.*" She coughs up the words in a rapid slur, speaking the truth before she can lose her nerve.

Julian doesn't glance over, doesn't look away from his careful navigation to Ellapond, but if the smirk tugging at his mouth means anything, he understood her perfectly.

When he drops a large warm palm high up on her leg, fingers curling to rest just too close to her inner thigh—it's a welcome brand.

"In that case, you're welcome to fall asleep anytime you want, Viv."

Chapter Twenty-Four

Viv:

Stop staring.

Viv:

Someone is going to notice.

Viv:

You're being obvious.

Jules:

No.

Jules:

Ignore Renee. You did wonderful today, Sugar Plum.

Jules:

I'm so proud of you.

Jules:

I'll see you after rehearsal. My place?

Viv:

You HAVE to stop staring.

Viv:

It's getting excessive.

Jules:

No.

Jules:

Timmer is staring.

Viv:

ALEX is my partner. He's supposed to stare.

Jules:

. . .

Viv:

DUET PARTNER

Viv:

You're literally our partnering instructor.

Viv:

You know he needs to watch me for timing.

Jules:

...

Viv:

what???

Jules:

You only have one partner, and we both know it's not that little boy.

Viv:

I didn't know Julian King gets jealous.

Jules:

Oh, I heard he gets more than just jealous.

Viv:

one image attached

Viv:

do you know how difficult it is to color match coverup to your legs?

Jules:

one image attached

Jules:

Use my card to order yourself more.

Or you could stop using me like a chew toy.

Order yourself more makeup, Sugar Plum.

Chapter Twenty-Five

Returning to rehearsing with Alex is fine, ideal even.

Vivian's injury—and subsequent inability to immediately jump back into trusting him—has put a damper on their burgeoning friendship. Rehearsal has been awkward, the time previously spent stretching and gossiping before and afterward is now filled with stilted silence and cordial—if not impersonal—nods. But it's fine. Awkward but fine.

When he lifts and spins her, it's always with a grip just shy of too tight, as if he's learned that his clammy hands were the original culprit and is trying to make up for it by squeezing her in a death grip. But it's fine. There are worse things than a partner with a firm grip.

What's not fine is the way Julian stares at her from across Studio C. The way his tongue peeks out to lick the corner of his lips before he corrects their steps. The way his hungry gaze meets her desperate one in the mirror. It's not fine at all.

It's tense—in decadent ways that remind her of teeth set against skin and obscene kisses. But it's also terribly distracting when Alex is standing at her shoulder, asking if she's ready to run through the variations again.

There are barely two weeks left until opening night. It's the worst time to be getting distracted. Not when there's still choreography to perfect and tech week to survive.

Too bad that no one told Julian. Vivian should be rehearsing extra. She should be running and stretching and rehabbing her shoulder, even though it's definitively healed by now. She should be prepping for tech and catching up with Scarlett and probably even trying to mend her friendship with Alex—if only to avoid visible tension onstage.

Instead, she's mentally reliving all her time spent with Julian like a slideshow of indulgence. Dangerous teeth. Messy hair. Strewn bedsheets. Midnight breakfast. Fingers crooked *inside of her* while she slept. Bite marks and bruises *everywhere*.

The dangerous soaring in her stomach from the way he gazes at her. The way he touches her. The things he whispered to her when he woke her up early, already thrusting into her as she fought off a blanket of sleep. Or the way he greets her at the door with a mind-melting kiss when she comes over after rehearsal. The way he never seems to stop staring.

Being a studio-length away from Julian and not eye-fucking him violently feels impossible. But ignoring his commanding presence is even harder.

"That's all for today," he says, breaking the insane way Vivian had been staring at his hands. Those hands and fingers that on countless occasions have—

Nope. Nope. No.

They are at Ellapond. Where they both work. Where he is her instructor. Where everyone thinks she's *nineteen*. Where coming clean about their—*Does a string of hookups that feel like* more *count as a relationship?*—relationship would mean admitting to lying at her audition.

All in all, Vivian's fucked.

Tech week starts so smoothly that Vivian never could have expected it would take a turn for the worse. Monday and Tuesday are practically perfect. She nails her duets, and the group numbers go off without a hitch. Music is cued on time, lighting changes are appropriately dramatic, and everything is perfect. Too perfect.

By Wednesday, things begin to unravel. First, a piece of the set breaks, a wooden board painted to depict a tree snapping clear in half. Then Ms. Renee decides to skip right over the seventh number, leaving Vivian scrambling to change costumes in the wings. Alex seems inexplicably cranky and practically refuses to meet Vivian's gaze after he's late to meet her for a set of assisted turns.

If Wednesday is messy, Thursday is downright disastrous.

"I know why you landed principal, and if you don't step down before opening night, everyone else will know too."

Vivian's in a mostly empty dressing room backstage, settling her frustrations by breaking in a new pair of pointe shoes. She's already cut, sewn, glued, and taped them to her liking, and now she's thwacking them against the concrete floor. Molding the shank and toe box until they reach the perfect midpoint of flexible but supportive.

Kelsey's looming over where Vivian sits in a dusty corner, supplies strewn about.

"Because I deserved it?" Vivian asks, already sick of this conversation. Since the very moment Kelsey first got in her way, stretching and glaring obviously, she's made it a point to stay out of the younger girl's way.

Jealousy is nothing new to Vivian, despite historically being on the other end of it. Finding ballet in middle school means that she's always been behind the curve.

Always coveted the head start other dancers have on her. Between her relative inexperience and financially modest upbringing, she's always had to work harder, do more with less. She tries her best not to let her jealousy bubble over into resentment, but it's clear that Kelsey doesn't share the same beliefs.

"Because you're a fucking slut," Kelsey bites out under her breath. She fusses with her bun, staring into one of the mirrors at a dressing table.

"Excuse me?" Vivian squawks. There's no love lost between the two girls, but Vivian didn't predict an escalation quite so dramatic.

"Yeah, that's right," Kelsey taunts. "I don't know how you got to Mr. Julian so quickly, but that *has* to be why he cast you. God knows it wasn't for your performance. I just don't know how he got Ms. Renee on board."

Something twisted and ugly churns in Vivian's stomach, a physical manifestation of fear and insecurity. She *knows* that Julian didn't cast her because they were sleeping together because when she auditioned back in August, they *weren't*. But that doesn't mean he hasn't given her preferential treatment since the nature of their relationship changed . . .

And it also doesn't mean they won't both lose their jobs if Kelsey opens her big mouth. Kelsey telling Ms. Renee about their relationship would mean trouble for Julian if everyone thinks Vivian is a teenager or trouble for Vivian if they find out she isn't. If Kelsey tells Ms. Renee—or anyone at all—they're *fucked*.

"I have no idea what you're talking about. You really shouldn't spread rumors," Vivian bluffs, operating purely on instinct.

"Oh, that's cute. You don't believe me?" The younger girl scoffs before she says the three words that ruin everything. "I. Saw. You."

Even spoken softly, Kelsey carefully enunciates so that Vivian can't miss a word.

They've been careful, so careful, but no one is perfect. Liquid ice runs through Vivian's body, an instant spike of fear.

"What do you want?" she asks, knowing that denial is no longer a feasible solution. She thought they'd been careful, but from the glint in Kelsey's eyes, it's clear that the other girl knows *something.*

"Cancel your audition with Renaissance."

"Cancel what audition?" Vivian stares up at Kelsey, pointe shoe heavier than a brick where it's forgotten in her lap.

"Don't play dumb. If I'm auditioning, I'm sure *he* secured you one as well. Cancel it." Kelsey finally turns a brown-eyed glare on Vivian, peering down at her over the nose she's caked in too-yellow foundation.

It's a shame to see such venom in a dancer so young. A shame that Kelsey is already so jaded and hateful.

"I have no idea what you're talking about, Kelsey. I don't have any auditions scheduled."

The delight that sparks in Kelsey's expression is dangerous, the grin of a predator as it corners its prey.

"Oh, really?" She laughs, but it rings through the dressing room sound closer to the cackle from an evil witch. "Guess he saw through you sooner than expected."

"Viv, do you mind if we run the woodland number again? Ms. Renee wants to try something different with the spotlight." Alex appears in the doorway moments later, red hair askew as though he's been ruffling it impatiently.

"Break a leg, *Viv*," Kelsey says, flitting around Alex and exiting the room, a smug expression cemented on her face.

The irony of waiting for Julian in the parking lot of El-lapond—the first place they met—isn't lost on Vivian. It seems fitting that she should ask him about Kelsey's comments in the same place that he first accused her of trespassing. Something about coming full circle and the balance of right and wrong echoes in Vivian's mind as her pulse races while she waits for Julian.

Chapter Twenty-Six

Julian beckons her into his car with a quick jerk of his chin. As much as her stomach is doing backflips, she knows better than to argue with him and risk someone seeing the two of them meeting at night. In the parking lot. Notably *alone*. And anyway, it's raining, so she doesn't want to stand in a dark, cold, wet parking lot while learning that—her lover?—Julian is a liar. Just like her.

As he always does, Julian manages to intuit her mood from a quick analysis of her expression and demeanor. It's all in the way her fingers are twisting in her jacket sleeves, the way she's absentmindedly chewing at her bottom lip.

"What is it, Viv?" It's the first thing he's said to her since Vivian climbed into the passenger seat of his car, only to find that he'd already turned on the seat warmer. The simple, thoughtful gesture tastes like ash in the wake of the lies and mystery Kelsey has brought to light.

Her hearts pounding, faster than it was on stage during tech. Faster than when she first auditioned for Ellapond only twelve weeks ago. Almost as fast as the evening he cradled her in his lap in Studio C.

"What's Renaissance and why does Kelsey want me to cancel my audition?"

"Before she was in administration, Maureen used to dance. A few years back, she and Renee started Ellapond with a third partner."

"I didn't know Ellapond had three founders."

"It was years ago, before I was touring with Pinsa."

When they're together, it's often all too easy to forget their age difference but every reminder is startling. To think that he's had a professional career since before she learned first position is often more than Vivian can wrap her mind around.

"The third founder was also their principal. She sprained her ACL two days before opening night of *La Lumière Du Jour.*"

Vivian winces in sympathy. As frustrating as her shoulder dislocation was, the timing, at least, didn't affect the performance. She hated sitting on the sidelines, but at least she was injured early enough into the schedule that it didn't affect her role or casting.

"Instead of just pulling in the swing for opening night and putting her on medical leave, they recast her role entirely. Maureen said that if she was younger and thinner, she wouldn't have been injured."

Vivian fights a gasp, knowing it would sound overly dramatic in the tense air of Julian's car. Dance is a world of drama and backstabbing but to hear of it retold this way seems so startlingly . . . *cruel.* So blatantly mean. Even after being on the receiving end of Maureen and Adelina's scrutiny, she can't imagine ever spitting such vitriol at another person.

"But she was a founder too." It's not quite a statement, not quite a question. Vivian can't help but vocalize her confusion.

"She was, but it was two against three. And without a role, she didn't want to stay on as a silent partner. Maureen and Renee outvoted her at every turn."

"So, she left?"

"She didn't have much of a choice. Maureen and Renee never outgrew their love of pettiness and high school grudges. At twenty-seven, she had trouble finding a new studio to take her. She could hardly list Maureen or Renee as a reference, and she'd spent the last few years of her career with Ellapond. They practically blacklisted her. She—" Julian breaks off, voice thick and choked.

"No one knew at the time, but she . . . she ended up in the hospital after passing out during an audition. She couldn't make herself younger, but she could be smaller. She was just skin and bones."

Julian doesn't have to say the words. He doesn't have to name the demon that haunts troubled dancers. The demon that tells them to skip lunch, to eat smaller portions, to train harder, to warp their bodies into impossibly sculpted lines. The devil that takes the faces of women like Maureen and Adelina, plucking at thin skin and harping on meal plans. Naming the demon doesn't make it easier to vanquish.

"But Maureen doesn't even dance anymore. They pushed out their principal when she got hurt, but Maureen doesn't even dance!" Frustration for this unnamed woman bubbles out of Vivian in sharp words.

Julian sighs, pulling his hat off and carding long fingers through his curls.

"I can't explain why Maureen and Renee were so cruel. Hypocrisy doesn't follow logic."

He sets his hat on the dashboard thoughtlessly. It's slightly damp from the rain and Vivian stares at it for far too long.

What if her shoulder had been worse?

"C'mere," Julian says in a hoarse voice before pulling his hand from its home on her thigh. And then he's fiddling with the handle on the car seat, pushing it as far from the dashboard as it will allow. With firm hands under her armpits, Julian hauls her right out of her seat and onto his lap as if she's a child in need of comfort. She's not sure which of them is more in need of physical reassurance. Her knee is digging into the seat belt anchor, and she's far too close to Julian for how violently her pulse is pounding. It shouldn't be hot.

"Is that why you were so weird about my sling and about private rehearsals?" she asks is a small voice.

"Yeah, Viv. I would never let that happen—" Julian's voice breaks off, thick with emotion. She hears what he doesn't say.

I would never let that happen to you.

His car is silent for several minutes, the air sticky with regret and lies.

"So, where do you come in?" Vivian's heart is thumping out of her chest, battering against the bones of her ribcage, demanding answers and resolution.

"After she recovered, Ella and I started a new studio—"

"Wait, Ella like Ellapond? And you have a studio?"

Julian laughs, but the sound is sharp and warped, more acerbic than humorous. "Yeah, they drove out the *named* founder of Ellapond. Fucked up, right?"

Vivian can only nod stiffly, mind whirring with information. When Kelsey said Vivian needed to cancel her audition, she thought . . . she's not sure what she thought, but she didn't expect *this*. This tale of an injured woman further wounded by Renee and Maureen. An injured woman betrayed by her colleagues. Her *cofounders*. Though Vivian is merely their principal dancer and not their cofounder, this could have easily been her. *She* could have been the rising star with her dreams quickly shattered, thanks to a simple injury.

"So, I've been recruiting from within Ellapond for Renaissance Ballet. Scarlett, Devonne, Paige," he says with a wince. He pauses, fingertips tightening where his hand rests in its customary place on her thigh. "Hopefully, you."

"You know that's fucked up, right? I mean, what Renee and Maureen did is horrible but so is poaching their dancers out from under them."

When Julian shrugs, his fingers flex and release. "If they could blacklist and bully their principal dancer—one of their *founders*—then they're a toxic danger to any of their dancers. Especially their newest principal."

And maybe Julian has a point there. For all that he's been recruiting behind their back, a studio run with his stern but honest instruction is certainly a safer environment for dancers than the one they've both been suffering through. He may be stern and grumpy, but he's never pinched at the skin of Vivian's waist during a costume fitting while judgmentally asking if she expects to be *this large* on opening night. He's never remarked on how *good* her petite frame looks on stage next to Alex's slender one. He's never dismissed her concerns as unimportant when she brought up *weeks* of missing paychecks. Not once has Julian ever implied that her fall from Alex's lift was because she was *too heavy*.

It's startling how easy complacency can be. How comfortable it is to continue with the status quo, avoiding dissent and discontent. How one day the right interaction, or the right words, can serve as the shocking wake-up call to shed a critical eye on your surroundings.

Vivian hasn't had enough experience as a professional dancer to know what her work environment is "normally like," but she knows enough to realize that this isn't it. The cost of walking in off the street to be cast as principal is that the gold pedestal she's let Ms. Renee place her on truly sits inside of a cage.

"So all this time you've been recruiting for Renaissance and you never said *anything*?"

After only a couple weeks together, Vivian understands why he didn't reveal this secret earlier. It doesn't stop the sting of hurt she feels at the slight. After all the secrets she's spilled to him, she wishes he'd felt ready to trust her with this one.

"Stop," he says, voice firm. "I was waiting until after next week to tell you. Even if you desperately deserve better than Ellapond, you deserve to have the opening night of your dreams. I didn't want to ruin your focus."

"And you still planned to steal me away for Renaissance after?" From her place on his lap, they sit eye to eye. Julian's hazel gaze is warm and unwavering.

"Viv, I'm not stealing you for Renaissance. I'm stealing you for me."

Warm hands slip under her jacket and over her leotard-covered waist. Vivian hates that the spandex material is stopping her from feeling his palms directly on her skin.

"What about Kelsey then?" All at once, the dread that was overshadowed by the truths of Ellapond's third founder comes rushing back, a flood of ice water down her spine. Vivian shivers in Julian's lap, goosebumps chafing against her leotard. "She said she knows. I didn't say anything, but she told me to cancel my audition. I can't believe that you're poaching her. She's blackmailing me!"

"I'll deal with Kelsey," Julian says with a sigh.

Vivian scoffs, puffing air against his chest. It's what she wanted to hear—that he would take care of it—and yet it doesn't bring her nearly the comfort expected.

"You'll 'deal with her?' Are you going to tell me you're in the mob next? Don't . . . hurt her, okay? She's a bitch, but she's only a girl."

The expression he levels at her is full of mild annoyance. "Hurt her? Who exactly do you think I am?"

Vivian rolls her eyes, pushing a little at Julian's chest where he's done his best to eliminate any of the distance between them. "Well, you sure seem to like hurting me . . ."

Warm breath fans her face before Julian is forcefully tucking her under his chin. "I'm sorry, Viv. I really am. I never could have seen you coming."

The car is quiet again. She doesn't know what to say. Doesn't know how to verbalize all the emotions rushing through her veins and coating her throat in tears.

I'm sorry I started all this by lying.

I hate what they did to Ella.

I don't know what I would have done without you.

I hate that you lied.

Who is Ella, and why were you willing to risk everything for her?

When the silence is so thick that Vivian is almost choking, she speaks, "Have you known Ella long? You two must be close to prompt such an elaborate revenge plot."

"You don't need to be jealous," he answers, giving absolutely no information away.

"I didn't say I was jealous," Vivian corrects quickly.

Julian snorts, and a puff of air tickles the baby hairs touching her forehead. "Relax, Sugar Plum. Ella's my sister. You'll meet her at your audition in a few weeks."

Chapter Twenty-Seven

As much as Vivian knows that Julian avoided telling her about Renaissance and Ella to avoid ruining her time in the spotlight, the news changes her all the same.

She's never had a *real* opening night before, so there's no true basis for comparison. But the first performance of *Le Pinson* isn't the magic she'd hoped for. The lighting and music run smoothly. Alex doesn't fumble any of the lifts. Their pas de deux runs smoothly, and besides a small wobble during a full-company number, opening night goes off without a hitch.

But with her rose-colored glasses removed, it's so apparent to see everything she's been missing. The way Ms.

Renee and Maureen whisper backstage during her quick change between numbers. The harsh eyes they cast on the younger dancers in the corps.

When Vivian first joined Ellapond, she was full of excitement and opportunity. Now, the sight of Ms. Renee or Kelsey brings her dread and regret. How could she have not known? How did she miss the signs?

Aside from quick glances backstage or charged nods during intermission, she doesn't see Julian at all for the first two weeks of performances. He's not avoiding her—he's been texting her daily—but she might be avoiding him. It's not until the third week of performances that he sends her a text she can't avoid.

Jules:

> R&M will offer to renew your contract this week. Ask for a copy to review but don't sign it.

Anxiety roils in Vivian's stomach as a living thing when she reads the message. It's not that she wants to stay. She can't now that she knows the truth. But there's no backup plan. Ellapond had been her Hail Mary pass. Her big break. Knowing what she does about Ms. Renee and Maureen, it's unlikely that they'll pass on a good word if she tries to look elsewhere. And for all his daily texts and meaningful glances, there's been no word from Julian about Ella or Renaissance since the night they spoke in his car during tech week.

Vivian:

> I don't have anything else lined up.

She hopes he'll read between the lines. If she leaves Ellapond without another studio or job lined up, she can wave goodbye to her chances at leaving behind her studio on Glenmarie Street.

Julian:

I just need a little more time.

Julian:

Please trust me.

When Maureen emails her about scheduling a time to come in and renew her contract, Vivian takes a leap of faith.

The afternoon of the final performance of *Le Pinson* rolls in with a sharp knock on her door that Vivian would know anywhere. It's the same knock she's been hoping for and dreading for weeks.

Julian, handsomely bundled into a winter coat with a high collar, stares at her from the doorway. And then he does the thing that never fails to rearrange her universe. He grins down at her, teeth gleaming and brown curls lightly dusted with snow. Vivian's heart flip-flops in her chest.

"I missed you, Sugar Plum."

"You have the two-thirty audition slot, but I want to show you around first," Julian says as he drives them to the building that houses the newly-renovated studios of Renaissance Ballet.

Despite her—admittedly feeble—protests, Vivian spent the week after closing *Le Pinson* with Julian. At his apartment.

Vivian tried to be mad at him. She really did. But Julian's explanation of needing to carefully coordinate her departure from Ellapond, his failure to renew his own contract with Renee, and Kelsey's audition and subsequent rejection from Renaissance . . . well, he made some pretty good points. And when he dropped to his knees and edged her with his mouth until she cried? That was fairly convincing too.

So when he packs her into his car the Tuesday after a week of bliss for her audition with Renaissance, she's barely worried. Hell, she's more nervous to meet Ella—his *sister*—than she is to audition. If she's survived a season with Maureen, Renee, and Adelina, she's confident that she can survive an audition anywhere. Even if Ella doesn't cast her, she'll survive. She doesn't want to rely on Julian for referrals, but she's confident that he can at least tell her which ballet companies are worth researching and which should be written off immediately.

Pulling into the parking lot of Renaissance Ballet sends a skitter of déjà vu up Vivian's spine. Seventeen weeks after first stumbling out of her car and into Ellapond, parking lots have come to hold more significance than they deserve. But from her first step into Renaissance's lobby, with its deep jewel-toned walls and attentive receptionist, it's clear that this is nothing at all like Ellapond.

For one, Julian is at her side, her dance bag slung over one shoulder with his other arm wrapped warmly around her.

He nods, introducing her to the receptionist, Hailey, before ushering her beyond the lobby for a tour. In the hour before her audition, they peek through the windows of several studios to watch rehearsals, visit his office, and scope out the stock room that's full of more shoes and supplies than Vivian could ever dream of.

"There's one more place I want to show you," Julian says, tugging her down a hallway to a set of tan double doors.

"This is the café."

The café is empty of dancers and food, but a long lunch counter sits on one side with small tables and booths scattered throughout the rest of the space. One full wall is lined with windows that showcase a snowy courtyard with benches and more tables beyond.

"Dancers are welcome to leave for lunch breaks as they please," Julian says as Vivian studies the space. The walls, tables, and fixtures are rich with color and texture without leaving her overwhelmed. The booths boast pillows and fluffy-looking cushions. There's a corner nook with a small electric fireplace that Vivian can already imagine cozying up to while reading before rehearsal or killing time next to while Julian's in a meeting.

"Once a month, we plan to bring in a nutritionist. There will be an opportunity to sign up for meetings with her in advance. If there's enough interest, we'll bring her in more often." Julian says it all with a small smile and a self-conscious shrug.

"It was important to both of us that we provide dancers *and* staff with the best resources possible," says a feminine voice from behind him.

The woman who walks into the café is undoubtedly Ella. From the long, graceful limbs and brown curls that she shares with her brother, the two could pass for twins.

"Hi," Vivian squeaks out. She'd prepared to meet Ella at the audition, but she hadn't prepared to meet her *here*, while she's in the midst of ogling their new café.

"Hi, Vivian. It's so lovely to meet you." The smile on Ella's face is bright and genuine.

"Ella, meet my girlfriend, Vivian," Julian adds with a smirk.

"Oh, we're dating now?" Vivian can't help but ask.

"Sugar Plum, we've been dating for weeks. You don't remember agreeing when I did that thing with my—"

Vivian practically vaults over a small table in an effort to clap a palm over Julian's mouth. It's one thing to meet the intimidatingly attractive sister of your intimidatingly attractive boyfriend; it's another thing to have him publicly remind you of the ways your brain turns to putty when he's around.

"That's enough, thank you," she says primly. She swats him in the chest before turning away dismissively. Ella is hiding a smile behind her hands when Vivian glances her way.

"Should we get on with this audition or what?"

Ella doesn't go easy on her. She doesn't let Vivian half-ass her audition just because she's dating the cofounder, and Vivian respects her all the more for it.

She also doesn't make Vivian wait for an answer.

"I'd like to cast you as a soloist," Ella starts, even as Vivian's still hunched over, palms on her knees, catching her breath. "I know you were principal at Ellapond, but I'm trying to run things differently here."

Vivian's stomach sinks into her knees. She didn't expect preferential treatment, but she didn't expect the opposite either.

"No." Ella is quick to interrupt her emotional spiral. "Don't panic. I'm not casting *any* principals yet. Auditions are still open, and I want to be able to pull different dancers for principal for different shows. Each show will have new choreography, and we'll hold internal auditions with the soloists to cast principals for each show. It's going to make seasons longer, but it means that principal will go to the dancer most suited to the choreography and performance."

Despite being different from all the casting methods that Vivian's familiar with, it sounds shockingly . . . fair.

When she tells Ella as much, the other woman chuckles out a laugh that's all regret and no humor.

"I know Jules has told you a bit about my time with Ellapond. He doesn't know it all, and I hope he never does. While there's no doubt that what Maureen and Renee did was cruel, I wasn't kind to myself either. I love ballet—in the heartbreaking, electrifying way that I suspect you do too. That's why it's so important to me that we run Renaissance differently. I won't make the same mistakes they did, and I won't allow young dancers to fall prey to their own insecurities the way I did. So auditions will be different and the environment will be different, but . . . "

Ella takes a deep breath, and Vivian can see the emotion shining in her eyes.

"Renaissance Ballet is different, but I hope you'll take a chance on us."

Epilogue

It becomes a poorly kept secret around Renaissance that a locked door means *don't knock*.

The first time Marin, the lead choreographer with a perpetually mild expression, walks in on them, they aren't even doing anything worth mentioning.

Yes, Julian came to collect Vivian after rehearsal. And yes, he did manage to end up seated on the ground, strong fingers digging into the arch of her left foot as she sighed. And, okay, yes, Vivian may have moaned, "Oh, please don't stop," a time or two. But it was a foot massage—really!

The second time, when Scarlett walks into Julian's office without knocking to find Vivian on his lap, practice skirt hiking up to her hips, she lets out a shrill squeak and trips over herself in an effort to escape before they're all scarred for life.

The third time, they're tucked into a corner booth in the café. It's late afternoon, so the space is mostly empty, the lunch hour having come and gone. Both of Julian's hands are visible—for a change—but when Ella approaches them to ask Julian about a discrepancy in the supply order, Vivian's hands are notably hidden from view.

"Can you two *please* get a room?" she begs.

They learn to lock the door.

"Well, Ms. Ladoe," Julian begins, sweeping into the nearly empty studio with a confidence in his stride that should be silly. It's hot as hell instead. "I'm afraid your performance today wasn't nearly up to par. I think it's time we consider . . . private lessons."

For all that Vivian wants to laugh at the blatant power dynamics of his setup, there's a shiver along her skin that she can't resist.

"Oh, no. I'm so sorry, *Mister* Julian. I didn't mean to disappoint you," she replies with a flutter of her eyelashes. It feels over the top and silly, but in a vibrant, playful way. "But I'm not sure that I can afford private lessons. They must be *so* expensive. I'm too young to get a job, but would you let me pay . . . some other way?"

"Fucking hell, Viv." Julian barks out a laugh, easily breaking character. It bounces through the studio, and

Vivian's jealous that she can't hoard it for herself. "Too young for a job? I think we're both past you being 'too young,' huh?"

Vivian grins at him mischievously. "Fine, you're right. Would you lock the door and get over here?"

By the time he's locked the studio door and turned to cross the room to her, Vivian's back in character.

"I'm just so busy with rehearsal, sir. If there's any way you could help me, I'd be . . . *so* . . . appreciative."

The closer Julian gets, the more her skin tingles, static electricity and goosebumps prickling her skin.

"I suspect we can come to some kind of arrangement, Ms. Ladoe," he rumbles out.

Before she can reply—in truth or in character—Julian wraps a large warm palm around the back of her neck, spearing fingers into the neat hair below her bun before he *pulls*.

Both Vivian and the shy, innocent *Ms. Ladoe* gasp, immediately wanting more. With a few more tugs, and the light *tink* of bobby pins dropping to the floor, Julian has dismantled her bun entirely.

"Fuck, Viv," he groans, leaning down to press his face into her blonde waves. "Why are you so short?"

"I'm not. You're just too tall!" she counters, grasping at his arms and shirt eagerly.

"C'mere," he says before he's hauling her off her feet and over to the side of the room. He props her up to sit on the barre where it's mounted to the wall. She's crowded into the corner of the studio, with a wall of barre on her right, a wall of mirror on her left, and a delicious looming

Julian before her. Seated on the barre, she's higher than him.

"Oh, this is perfect. Why haven't we done this before?" he asks. He's eye level with her breast and quickly tugs the straps of her leotard off her shoulders to reveal them.

Vivian wants to reply with something about privacy or professionalism or how *his sister* is her boss. But when his teeth catch around her nipple, all she manages is "Guhhhh—"

Julian wedges himself between her spread thighs, dropping a hand to her waist when she totters dangerously from her perch. He sucks and bites at her breasts, leaving a wake of raised red skin behind before he finally reaches up to take her mouth.

It's rare that Vivian is taller than Julian, and the height emboldens her in their kiss. Instead of allowing him to run the show, she meets him with force, licking when he licks, nipping when he nips. When he drops his mouth down to her neck, she's breathless and certain her lips are bruised.

"You did so good today, Sugar Plum," he croons against her damp skin. "I watched your rehearsal after my meeting. You've been working so hard, and it shows."

Vivian's skin flushes at the praise and her heartbeat ramps up.

"Nuhhh, thank you," she gasps out.

"Can you get undressed for me, sweetheart? I don't want to rip your leotard."

Vivian's panting above Julian's bent head, breath fanning his curls. "Gotta get down."

Once her feet touch the floor, Vivian's certain that she's never undressed quicker. Not even during quick changes backstage.

She glances around the room impatiently as Julian takes his own turn undressing. Aside from her bag and shoes in a cubby by the door and the AV equipment, the studio is empty from mats, furniture, and any other items that would make for a suitable surface.

"I don't think I should get back on the bar. I'll be too high, and it won't—"

Before she can finish, Julian's dragging her to the polished wood floor, right there in the corner by the barre and mirror.

"It's okay, Sugar. We're good right here," he says between kisses. "You're gonna be good for me right here. Isn't that right?"

Julian is splayed out on the studio floor, all strong, elegant limbs, brown curls, and playful hazel eyes. The floor of Renaissance Ballet—where they work and dance together every day. And after they finish debauching it, they'll go home. To Julian's townhouse—*their* home. Where Vivian gets to hear his toe-curling comments and ache from his delicious fingers whenever she wants. Where she's found a home beyond ballet in the person she'd least expected.

So she nods eagerly, desperate to be the good girl that she is and lets Julian pull her on top of him.

"Are you ready? I don't wanna rush you, but there is a community class booked in here soon."

"There's wha—" she tries to choke out, but Julian's swiping thick fingers against her.

"Oh, you're definitely ready. Will you ride me, sweetheart?"

He doesn't wait for her reply, taking his cock in hand to draw tight circles against her entrance, spreading her wetness. Julian lines them up and then Vivian's sinking down, down, down. Until she's so full that she might be more of him than she is of herself. More him than her. But then he'll be more her than him too.

He feels so stupidly perfect inside her that as soon as their hips are flush, she can't help but clench around him.

"Fuck, Viv. Sugar Plum, shit." Julian's babbling, firm hands supporting her hips as she writhes atop him, ever the accommodating throne. "You're perfect, sweetheart. I love when you ride me."

They're both panting, sweat slicking their palms and hips. It always seems impossible that Julian can get her there so quickly, and yet the way he always studies her with keen and careful eyes speaks of a man committed to memorizing her every desire.

"You're so perfect, sweetheart," he says again. "But we do have to make this quick. Ella will kill me if class starts late again."

It wouldn't be the first time they held up someone's schedule.

Vivian simply moans. Coherent words are deemed too much work.

"I'm sorry. I love you, Sugar Plum," Julian apologizes, and Vivian immediately knows what's coming.

"Oh, fuck, please. Love you too. *Pleasepleaseplease*," she slurs out, breathless.

Pain soars through her body as Julian's hand lands on her clit with a swift smack. She cries out something resembling his name when pain is quickly replaced by pleasure. Three more strikes and she's coming, clenching and grinding against him involuntarily.

They only spare five minutes to sprawl on the studio floor in sated exhaustion before dragging themselves into their clothes for the short drive home that would undoubtedly feel excruciatingly long.

And if the students of the community class arrive to find that a corner of the studio's mirror is covered in handprints and smudges . . . well, at least they locked the door.

Glossary

Arabesque: A ballet position in which the weight of the body is supported on one leg, while the other leg is extended in back with the knee straight.

Artist residency/Artist-in-residence: Artist residencies provide artists, performers, and creative professionals the time, space and resources to work, on the research and development of their practice outside of their typical environment. For performers, this may involve teaching or hosting workshops rather than performing.

Barre: A stationary handrail that supports dancers in ballet training and warm up exercises.

Chaînés: Chaînes turns are turns that are performed "in a chain" when a dancer lifts onto relevé and then pivots from side to side, traveling over a distance.

Corps de ballet: These are the lowest ranked dancers and are perform as the ensemble of a ballet company.

Cou-de-pied: A ballet position in which the arched working foot is raised to an open position in the air to rest in front of, behind, or wrapped around the ankle of the supporting leg.

Dance swing: An offstage performer who learns and rehearses multiple dance numbers and is ready to perform at a moment's notice. These performers typically learn multiple roles.

Glissade: A ballet movement in which a dancer extends one leg along the floor to the front, side, or back from a fifth position with the knees slightly bent, transfers their weight to the working leg and slides the other foot next to the first leg.

Jeté: A ballet leap where the weight of the dancer is transferred from one foot to the other.

Open audition: Casting calls that are open to any dancers who meet the criteria.

Pas de deux: A dance for two performers, typically a male and female. It is a characteristic of classical ballet and may be referred to casually as a duet. Pas de deux typically consist of five parts: the entrée, the adagio, two variations, and the coda.

Passé: A ballet movement in which the foot of the working leg passes the knee of the supporting leg from one position to another or one leg passes the other in the air or one foot is picked up and passes in back or in front of the supporting leg.

Pirouette: A ballet turn performed in place on one leg.

Pointe shoes: Ballet shoes designed with a box and platform at the toe of the shoe to allow dancers to perform on the tips of their toes. Dancers often cut, glue, scrape, mold and otherwise alter their shoes to suit their feet, style, and preferences. While construction varies between models and manufacturers, most pointe shoes have a shank, toe box, platform, vamp, sole, and ribbons.

Principal dancer: The highest ranked dancers in a ballet company. Principal dancers typically perform the leading roles in ballet productions.

Private audition: Where dancers are invited to audition by taking a company class and being seen by the ballet master and/or director.

Relevé: A ballet move that involves rising up onto the balls of the feet or the toes, either on one or both feet.

Retiré: A ballet position in which the thigh is raised to an open position in the air with the knee bent so that the pointed toe rests in front of, or behind or to the side of the supporting knee.

Soloist dancer: These dancers are ranked above the corps de ballet but below principal dancer(s). Soloists perform more leading roles and sections of dancing, including solos. They frequently as understudies for leading roles.

Tech week: Also called technical week. Tech week is the time to rehearse the full performance with all technical elements in place. It typically occurs the week immediately prior to opening night.

Acknowledgments

In a year where it felt like I held the concentrated attention of Murphy's Law, I could *never* have done this on my own.

To my core book besties, Steph, Maddi, and Vic: Without a doubt, I wouldn't have finished L&L without your support, patience, and friendship. Between help with marketing, keeping me organized, commiserating when life hit me hard, and so much more—thank you, thank you, thank you.

To Maddi: Thank you for the stellar edits and for sharing a single brain cell with me. You can never leave me.

To Zee: Thank you for your sass, proofreading, and infinite patience when I took forever to finish writing.

Thank you to Ruthie and Literary Media Tours for an amazing cover reveal and stellar ARC management.

A big thank you goes out to Semira and Kat for saving my butt when I frantically needed spicy feedback.

To T: I hope you don't read this, but if you do, infinite thank-yous for all of your graphics (and font, design, headshot, website, etc.) assistance.

To my husband: Thank you for being mine.

Finally, thank you to any reader who takes a chance on *Leaps & Lies*.

About the Author

After countless stories scribbled in notebooks that will never see the light of day, Ada decided it was time to brave the world of publishing. While *Leaps & Lies* is her debut release, it certainly won't be her last!

Find her online at @authoradavane or ada-vane.com.